Out of the Depths

A.S.Chambers

Acknowledgements

Many thanks to the long-suffering artistic genius that is
Liam Shaw for his awesome artwork and also to Wayne
Ashworth for his helpful hints regarding parks where lovers
of days gone by may have visited in Preston.

A special thank you to my following Book Club members
for their dedicated support:
Paul Lewis, Gemma Innes, Kevin Denwood and
Jacob Matts

Also, a shout out to the following Kickstarter backers in
helping this book reach publication:
Sergey Kochergan, Francesco Tehrani, Ron Chick, Debs,
Rebecca Armstrong, Simon Brindley, Anthony Holmes and
Bec Pearce

Also by A.S.Chambers

Sam Spallucci Series.
The Casebook of Sam Spallucci - 2012
Sam Spallucci: Ghosts From The Past - 2014
Sam Spallucci: Shadows of Lancaster – 2016
Sam Spallucci: The Case of The Belligerent Bard - 2016
Sam Spallucci: Dark Justice – 2018
Sam Spallucci: Troubled Souls - 2020
Sam Spallucci: Bloodline - Prologues & Epilogue – 2021
Sam Spallucci: Bloodline – 2021
Sam Spallucci: Fury of the Fallen – 2022
Sam Spallucci: Lux Æterna – Due 2023

Short Story Anthologies.
Oh Taste And See – 2014
All Things Dark And Dangerous – 2015
Let All Mortal Flesh – 2016
Mourning Has Broken – 2018
Hide Not Thou Thy Face – 2020
If Ye Loathe Me - 2022
Hear My Scare - Due 2025

Ebook short stories.
High Moon - 2013
Girls Just Wanna Have Fun – 2013
Needs Must - 2019

Novellas.
Songbird – 2019
Bobby Normal and The Eternal Talisman - 2021
Bobby Normal and the Virtuous Man - 2021
Bobby Normal and the Children of Cain - 2022
Bobby Normal and the Fallen - Due 2023
Child of Light - Due 2023
Child of Fire - Due 2024

Omnibuses.
Children of Cain - 2019
Macabre Collection: Volume One - 2022
Macabre Collection: Volume Two - 2023
Sam Spallucci Omnibus: Volume One - 2022
Sam Spallucci Omnibus: Volume Two - Due 2023

Contents

Family History

If there is such a place as Hell, Robert Richmond, renowned archaeologist, considered, *then this must surely be it.*

As some young girl, whom he reckoned hadn't eaten a square meal in about six months, prattled on to the host of the late-night chat show about how she was doing *her bit* to prevent the genocide of a native population in a small African country, the name of which she couldn't even pronounce (every time she flipped the consonants, Richmond felt the surfaces of his molars grind down just a bit more), the bearded archaeologist sat thinking that he could be somewhere else.

I could be at home, feet up, fire roaring, fine brandy in hand, listening to some Mahler, he thought. *The fifth. That would certainly hit the spot. Even if it was ripped off by that chap for that bizarre television programme. God knows why Sylvia insisted we watch it. It was total nonsense.*

Yes. Mahler's fifth. That would do the trick. That opening brass: slow, restrained, rising in a crescendo; the clash of the cymbals; the feel of dread as it dies back down. Perfection.

The part of the eminent academic's brain that had been keeping tabs on the banality of the conversation around him registered that someone had asked him a question. With the well-practised skills of someone who has spent numerous years on this planet having to inter-act with those individuals who possessed an intelligence which was a minuscule fraction of his, he answered without hesitation, "Well, I am sure that the young lady on my left here feels that by buying cruelty-free *lippy* from some hipster hut on the high street is the *only* thing she can do to protect an indigenous culture from being erad-icated, but I think people need to take far more direct ac-tion."

Some uptight chap sporting a black roll-neck and a waxed Van Dyke leaned forward, his over-sincere brown eyes peering at Professor Richmond through his retro, heavy-framed spectacles.

Does the esteemed Professor think... Richmond began to predict internally.

"Does the esteemed Professor think,"

...without the shadow of a doubt...

"without the shadow of a doubt,"

...that someone whose work dwells on the dim, dis-tant past...

"that someone whose work dwells on the dim, dis-tant past,"

...has any justification commenting on the here and now?

"has any justification commenting on the here and now?"

Dear God, these idiots were so damned predict-able.

"It is my unquestionable belief that history certainly has a habit of repeating itself."

"Oh, and you find that, do you? Digging about in your dirty little holes?" the bespectacled fool, who could only be a sociologist, sneered.

"Sonny, if you knew what I found whilst digging in my dirty little holes, your pathetic little attempt at facial hair would turn white overnight."

"Professor Richmond! Professor Richmond! Are you down there?"

"Well, where else would I bloody be?" The archaeologist leaned back against the smoothly hewn wall of the expanded trench. Damn it was hot! Infernally hot. It was as if the devil himself was here, stoking the coals of his eternal furnace. He stared down the line of local workers who were carefully teasing the compressed silt of the old riverbed away from the tantalising shapes contained within. This was going to be a big one, he knew it in his gut. As soon as the tech chappies had said that there were anomalies, a *lot* of anomalies here, all packed in together, he had made the call to dig deep down the side of whatever was lurking under the compacted silt and go in laterally. The technique was far from being an accepted manner of excavation, but he knew, down in his gut, that it was the right move. The silt would be a pain to excavate from on top. It would be like trying to dig on shifting sands and there was a terrible risk of damaging whatever was hidden beneath. Whereas, if they came in at it from the sides, any slippage would come down to where they were digging from. They just had to be careful that the whole lot didn't decide to shift.

Mind you, he considered, *it's been there for about*

three thousand years. I can't see it being in a hurry to go anywhere else right now. Probably comfortable where it is.

"Professor Richmond!" came the frantic shout, once again. "Did you hear me?"

Richmond closed his eyes and sighed. "Eugene!" he bellowed up from the excavation. "A deaf wombat that was deep in its antipodean nest could hear your incessant whining." Wiping sweat from his forehead and opening his eyes, he asked, "What the hell is it, man?"

"It… it's your wife, sir. *Mrs* Richmond."

"Jupiter's eyes, I know what my wife is called. What about her?"

"She's on the phone."

This pulled him up short. He checked his watch, wiping powdery dust from the glass in order to inspect the local time. It was just gone six in the evening here, so would be just after two back in Oxfordshire. He frowned. Sylvia never rang during the day. She knew not to interrupt him.

Which meant it could only be one thing.

"Keep working in," he instructed the team's foreman. "Once you reach something of note, wait for me. I'll be back as soon as I can." Heaving his bulk up the rickety wooden ladder that was the only access into the deep excavation, he climbed up into the early evening of the Indus Valley. "Did she say what it was?" he asked of the small, rat-like man in the ill-fitting work clothes that scurried along behind him, back to the main tent of the dig site. Eugene had come highly recommended by a mutual acquaintance as the sort of personal assistant that everyone needed. Richmond had decided after just a week, that the swine of a previous employer had actually wanted to be shot of the ineffectual moron but hadn't possessed the guts required to give him the shove. Well, he had no such squeamish hesitancy. Once they were back in England, Eugene was getting the old heave-ho. "How did she sound?"

The PA looked blankly up at his employer.

"My wife, damn it! How did she sound? Was she worried? Upset?"

"I… I… don't really know."

"Of course you don't," Richmond grumbled as he entered the control tent. "Your mother had your emotions snipped off with your umbilical cord." He snatched up the field telephone and shooed the little man out of the tent, sealing up the flap behind him, attempting a modicum of privacy. "Sylvia? It's me. What's wrong?"

"Robbie? Is that you? The line's awful."

"Yes, yes. It's me." He shifted position. They'd had terrible problems with tech ever since they'd pitched camp. None of the usual complicated stuff seemed to want to work. They'd managed to set up a very minimal internet connection as a lifeline to the outside world, but it only allowed the occasional email and was nowhere near stable enough for video calls. Fortunately, Richmond was a man who was always prepared for every eventuality so had dug out this old relic of a field telephone and, with a few prayers to the Almighty, it managed to work about seventy-five per cent of the time. Cradling the brown bakelite handset against his shoulder he spoke into the mouthpiece: "Can you hear me now? What's the matter?"

"Yes, dear. That's better." His wife paused. "It's Elle."

Why, oh why, do they have to insist on having soci-ologists on these damned things: Richmond lamented internally. *Seriously, they will be the death of us all.*

"Well, as I think you would be aware *Professor,* if you were to actually read recent academic writings which have shed immeasurable illumination on the workings of society, you would in fact see that…" The young man with the excuse for facial hair staggered to a halt as Richmond let out a bellow of a yawn. "I… I… must say…"

"Say what, sonny? You haven't actually *said* anything for the last five minutes. All you've done is regurgitate the words of funding-grabbing shysters who haven't once set foot outside of their academic ivory towers." Richmond shook his head. "I actually thought you were trying to do me a favour and providing a nice monotonous ineffectual drivel to aid my drifting off to sleep.

"However, it would appear that I was wrong.

"You are in fact a very, very *dangerous* individual, indeed.

"The trouble with you lot is that you've not had any new thoughts in over fifty years. You *say* that you have. You scribble things down in your little publications, give them fancy new titles and slap each other on the back in congratulations. But, in reality, all you *actually* do is sit in front of your little screens scrolling through the texts of what the last idiot has written, then note down the complete opposite. You have no empirical research to back it up whatsoever.

"And why is that? Post-modernity — everything is wrong. Nothing can be proven. Dear Lord, it's no wonder the world is in such a state. You think it's all a game, sitting there, writing down impressive words and humorously slagging each other off. Well, let me tell you this, *boy*, every word we say, every sentence we write, has re-percussions, and you lot have damned a whole genera-tion to the fiery pits of Tartarus. You have given politicians free rein to do whatever they want, because you've basic-ally said, "No one can be trusted, so what the hell?" As a result, we've ended up with power-hungry monsters in charge, grabbing whatever they can to feather their own gold-lined nests. But, not only that, the populace has been brainwashed into believing that it is more impotent than a Sultan's chief eunuch. The common people have been taught to accept that whomever they put in power will do just the same. Hell, Jesus Christ could come back today, run for global president, and the first thing the voters would say is, 'Well, what's his game then? I don't like him. Can't trust blokes with beards.'"

Richmond paused as he stroked his own shaggy facial hair.

"No, let me tell you, even half a century ago, the populace would not have stood for the grief that the *idiocracies* of today deal out. The masses would have clamoured until the bloated, over-stuffed politicos scampered from their houses of power with their tails between their legs. And as for a few hundred years ago? There would have been heads rolling. Then as for a few *thousand* years back…?

"Well, I think what I've seen there would seriously turn your stomach."

As the man of just sixty mortal years stood staring up at the imposing millennia-old figures in front of him, he felt as if every single second of every minute of every hour of every damned day was weighing upon his broad shoulders. Richmond dragged a folding chair towards him, leaving a pair of erratic tracks in the dirt. Positioning the seat in a convenient spot, he collapsed into its less-than-stable, creaking embrace.

The crew had been packed off for the evening and he was now alone with the harsh light of the field lamps illuminating the silent sentinels in front of him: tall clay statues that towered over the majority of those who had unearthed them from their long slumber.

Richmond had never seen anything like them. Not at all. Yes, the Harappan culture was renowned for its skilful art. The artefacts that Mackay and the like had unearthed back in the early to mid-twentieth century had already demonstrated that. However, it had always been very much small-scale stuff: seals, figurines, votives.

There had never been anything really monumental or grand scale. People just generally accepted that, for that period in ancient history, you had to look elsewhere: Egypt, Greece, the usual chappies.

Until now.

It was the discovery of a lifetime, guaranteed to firmly etch Richmond's name indelibly on the stone tablets of history.

Yet, as he sat staring up absentmindedly at the towering clay army in front of him, his mind was elsewhere.

Eloise.

He drew his emergency flask out of his jacket, unscrewed the cap and took a long swig of the expensive brandy.

Damn girl, he muttered internally. *So bloody strong-willed.* He allowed himself a small smile. *I wonder where she gets it from?*

His only child had always been what some had

called *feisty.* He preferred the term *single-minded.* To Richmond, this was not a problem, not at all. He had indeed encouraged it. So many damned parents hovered around their offspring like wretched helicopters, dipping and diving in whenever their progeny had the slightest stumble. The kids never learned how to stand on their own two feet. He had always been determined to produce a young woman who knew her own mind and was willing to do what was necessary to achieve what she wanted. He remembered the quests they used to go on around the grounds of the house when she was still in single digits. She would be dressed as the brave knight of the Round Table and he the lowly serf, ready to follow her orders. So many times they had chased after trails that were to lead them on quests for the Grail. As they adventured, he would enchant her with tales of Arthur and explain how myth had a basis in reality. Just because we could not comprehend what something meant in our modern age, did not mean that there was no basis in fact hundreds or thousands of years ago.

He remembered the first time she had gone on one of these quests on her own. He had been tied up with paperwork for some over-officious dean of some godforsaken department somewhere. When Eloise hadn't reappeared he had started to worry and had gone to look for her, eventually finding her curled up asleep under a hedge at the bottom of the garden.

"Daddy, I had the strangest dream," the little four-year-old had said as he had carried her back up to the house. He had thought at the time just how small and fragile his only child was.

Dear God, he could hardly say that of her now.

Wellington University! What the hell was she thinking? She was halfway through her first term at a far more respected establishment, acing all her assessments, and now she was talking about upping and leaving at the end of term, transferring to some tin pot little establishment just off the A45 in the arse end of beyond. Utterly ridiculous!

He decided that he would have to ring her once the time zones were more favourably aligned. Try to talk some sense into her.

"Good luck with that," Richmond muttered as he took another swig of the brandy.

He rested his head against the smooth wall of the compacted riverbed and let his eyes survey the figures in front of him that were clawing their way out of the excavation with their elongated, twisted limbs. They were pottery of some sort, but massive. The closest he could think of in size were the Terracotta Army. Most finds from this period were very much small-scale and for household use, but these chaps... These were like an army.

And one under attack, at that.

Whereas the Qin dynasty marvels were a band of noble soldiers standing tall, guarding their dead emperor's tomb, these monstrous chaps looked like they were having the devil beaten out of them. Their limbs were bent, twisted and articulated in a manner that suggested they had been fighting something from above. Their arms, for want of a better word, were thrust up above them as if they were protecting themselves from a bombardment, yet no weapons or projectiles had been as yet located.

The figures were in all manner of poses. Some were upright, some knelt, others almost completely obliterated. Yet they all shared a common pair of features: a minimal amount of facial detail; a distinct lack of hands.

Their heads were a kind of dome that rested upon their broad shoulders. There appeared to be neither nose nor eyes, just a wide gash from left to right in an approximation of a mouth. One had been uncovered that had its mouth open and a huge, serpentine tongue was emerging from the gash like a hungry creature writhing out of its lair in search of its prey. Richmond looked down at the prone figure and shuddered. It was quite ghastly.

As were the things that the creatures possessed instead of hands.

The archaeologist eased himself up from the camp seat and approached one of the statues. He took his brush from his back pocket and carefully stroked a fine layer of dust away from the surface of the smooth, deadly-looking lance that resided in the place of the being's hand. He ran his finger along the surface and marvelled at just how lustrous the polish was. Most pottery from this period was still quite crude in its finish. You could feel imperfections on the surface of most domestic pottery — small little dimples in the firing or runs in the glaze. It was incredibly rare to find anything but the higher echelons of society using pots with a fine lustre.

The finish on these was far superior to anything he had previously unearthed. The archaeologist stroked his beard and surmised that it must have been something in the firing process. Something to do with the heat.

But what the hell are they doing in a sodding river bed?

Were they ritualistic? A representation of something?

Something niggled at the back of his memory and he dug a book out of the breast pocket of his field jacket, thumbing through his varying hand-scrawled notes until he found what he was looking for.

"Floods great and may, compassed by the Dragon, thou badest swell and set free, O Hero.

"Strengthened by songs of praise thou rentest piecemeal the Dasa, him who deemed himself immortal."

Richmond tapped the notebook in his hand. Were these figurines meant to represent the Dasa? Were they supposed to be a demonic army that had been conquered by a hero unleashing the mighty waters? He lifted his eyes to study the layers that covered the figures. It was approximately twenty metres above them. Of that, the top five were stratified, showing the layers of the passing centuries, but the remaining fifteen were all solid in colour and texture. It was dark and the excavation had revealed ample remains of freshwater marine life.

In short, these chaps had been covered by a river in a single cataclysmic deluge.

There was a myth that the god Indra had burst the dams here, a notion poo-pooed by many. Perhaps they ought to reconsider their post-modern dismissal that a legend could have its roots in reality.

The stupid little sociologist with the pointless excuse for facial hair was shaking his head, a smug look on his face that felt almost as sincere as a politician visiting an amputee ward after selling the weapons that maimed them to the opposite side.

"Sonny, you look like you've just dealt then smelt the most amazing curry-enhanced fart that humanity has ever heard. Are you just going to sit there smirking or perhaps try to defend yourself? Did they teach you how to argue at your silly little public school that your parents paid for in order to get you out from under their feet, or were you too busy weeping into your pillow that the other boys didn't like you?"

The other academic stopped shaking his head and glowered at the archaeologist. The rest of the guests were seated in stunned silence. They all knew that, should they agree to appear on a show with the renowned Professor Robert Richmond, then they were to expect fireworks. He was always invited along for his volatile temper as well as his incisive academic mind. However, they were all currently thinking the same thing: *He's gone too far.*

"Dangerous?" It was one word. Small yet distinct. "You call me a dangerous individual?" The sociologist was leaning forwards, perched on the edge of his chair. "You call wanting to hone society down to its utter truth dangerous? You call wanting to eradicate all the prejudices of millennia of religion dangerous?" He gave his head another small shake. "Let me tell you what is *dangerous,* esteemed professor. Dangerous is spending a lifetime searching for something that does not exist. Dangerous is being obsessed that a fairy tale is a reality."

Richmond let out an exasperated sigh. "If you're talking about my research into Arthurian Legend and the Grail, then you truly have no idea what you are talking…"

"*Dangerous…*"

The other guests inhaled in shock as the sociologist cut Richmond off mid-flow. No one ever did that.

"… is leaving your family for months on end as you travel the globe in search of your precious little *archetype.* Dangerous is the amount of money that you have squandered from the purses of numerous universities as you continue to dig up nothing but dust from your dear little digs."

"That is just not the case. Only a few months ago we uncovered the Sentinels in Mohenjo Daro. They were acclaimed as…"

"*Dangerous* is putting your obsession before your family, your supposed loved ones. Dangerous is driving your daughter away so that she rebels and quits the university place that you arranged for her, running away to a smaller establishment of which you do not approve."

Richmond opened his mouth to speak but no words would come. He could not comprehend what had just happened. This horrid little man had suddenly made things incredibly personal. "What the hell are the affairs of my daughter to you?" he finally managed.

The sociologist leant back in his chair, a sly grin on his face. "Apparently they mean more to me than they do to you, Professor."

The camp bed was damned uncomfortable. Richmond tossed and turned, thumped his pillow, kicked at his sheets and finally just submitted to another disturbed night of staring up at canvas.

Half an hour of shouting followed by a month of silence.

How the hell had it come to this?

Damn the girl! How the Dickens could she think that concrete block which until the nineties had just been dishing out motor mechanics awards could provide a more *stimulating* course than one of the finest educational institutions in the world?

He had tried to explain that she was wrong, but she just wouldn't have it. She just wouldn't listen. Instead, she kept insisting that Wellington was *where she needed to be.* What the devil was *that* supposed to mean? He blamed all that wretched veganism and yoga rubbish. Filling her young head with all those stupid wishy-washy, namby-pamby ideas of self-discovery and unfolding of the inner self.

Just a lot of bloody long-haired hippies trying to get into each others' pants!

The furious father of the stubborn offspring closed his eyes again, trying to achieve his own state of bliss in order to ready himself for the final push tomorrow. It was almost December and the weather was turning as winter finally started to take hold. They would have to pack up in a week or so, handing the site over to the local authorities and bigwigs who would naturally try to claim all the credit for his team's discoveries.

Damned politics of academia! Ah well, he had the Castlerigg site to start work on in February. Richmond shuddered. The Lake District in late winter would be a chilly counterpoint to the balmy heat of summer and autumn spent digging in the Indus Valley. He seriously doubted that the excavation of a late-Neolithic stone circle would produce anything of the magnitude of the army of monsters that they had uncovered here.

Over two thousand!

Nothing of the like had previously been found in this neck of the woods. Not ever! Not only that but the sheer *vitality* of the creatures… No, the statues. He had to stop that. He kept referring to the figurines in his notes as if they were alive, and they weren't. They were just pottery, hardened clay. But, they were so lifelike, even with their blank, misshapen faces.

They were so… inexplicable.

Richmond opened his eyes, stroked his unkempt

beard and swung his already clothed legs out from under his sheets. He dragged on his shirt and jacket, heaved on his boots, grabbed a small torch and headed over to the dig site. If he couldn't sleep, he was damned well going to make good use of his time.

Just as he had this afternoon.

He had sacked Eugene.

Dear God, he'd never seen a man wail and weep so much in his life. You'd have thought that he had told the silly little sod to go home and shoot his ruddy goldfish! Well, at least that was one thing done. He had been packed off out of the site and sent on his merry way back to somewhere that Richmond couldn't give two hoots about.

However, as he descended one of now numerous decidedly unsteady ladders into the excavation, that did leave him in a certain predicament. He would now have to find another personal assistant, and good ones were few and far between. He set his feet down on the compacted riverbed and turned to face the army of creatures.

Not creatures; statues.

He wanted someone who showed initiative, not a mindless golem that had been constructed to just do as they were told, even when it was the wrong thing.

Richmond frowned and shuddered. Someone had walked a goose across his grave there. Shaking his head, he approached the broken, defeated army.

The last month had been incredibly productive. The old river had been completely cleared and the army stood exposed once more after a period of about three and a half thousand years. It was now possible to walk between the figures and, as one did, one really got a sense of what they were…

No. What they represented.

Killing machines. These were supposed to be things that were made for one purpose alone, to slaughter those that stood before them. Broad of shoulder and lofty of height, those that remained standing towered above the tallest members of the dig team. Not even that chap from Karachi, the one with the odd twitch, came close to them. Even those that had fallen or had been smashed under the weight of the water gave a casual observer a deeply unsettling feeling of dread.

Richmond paused, turned and frowned.

"Hello? Who's there?"

There was no reply from the depths of the petrified army. There was just a sixty-year-old man in a forest of clay.

Richmond frowned and continued with his inspection, shining his light over the lustrous sheen of the giants. No, he had never seen a finish such as this. It was unlike any recorded type of pottery and would no doubt cause argument and controversy when he published his findings. Some would call it an aberration, others a random act of geological interference.

Others would just say that he didn't know terracotta from porcelain.

He wouldn't care. He would write up his findings, know that he was correct, and move on.

Stuff the lot of 'em. Pompous idiots.

Richmond shone his light down between a row of fallen creatures in order to pick out the safest route and paused. Over to his left, he saw another flash of light. He twitched his own torch to see if it was a reflection off the glaze of the statues, but the light did not reappear. Frowning, he began to pick his way through the site. He had only progressed a few metres when the light flashed again, this time to his right. Richmond changed course and headed towards it. Was someone else down here?

"Hello?" he called out.

The light bobbed up and down again, this time hovering in view down a passageway of the long-dead sentinels.

Not dead; statues.

"Who's there?"

There was no reply. The light just seemed to hover quite a way away. It was hard to accurately judge the distance due to the dark of night.

Richmond continued to head towards it. When he reckoned he was about five metres away, the light moved. It started to head over to the side of the dig.

"Wait! Who's there?"

The light did not pause until it reached a ladder leading up to the surface. Richmond clambered across a number of fallen and smashed figurines until he reached the ladder and paused.

The light was there, but it was not coming from any torch. It was a small ball of luminescence, about the size of a tennis ball and it bobbed up and down by the ladder.

"What the devil?"

The glowing orb bobbed up and down again.

Richmond stood stroking his beard in wonder.

The orb dashed over from the ladder, spun three times around his head, then resumed its position at the base of the exit from the trench.

The bemused archaeologist shrugged and did as he seemed to be instructed. He began to climb the ladder out of the dig. The small orb flittered to and fro ahead of his ascent until he reached the surface and then it darted off in front of him. He had come to the surface just by the remains of the main gate of the city. The orb sped through the gap in the ruined walls then turned back and bobbed up and down impatiently.

Richmond gave a quick glance back across the vast ceramic army before following after his curious little guide. It dodged and darted through the well-known streets upon which Richmond had walked many times in his numerous visits here and, as their journey progressed, it easily dawned upon him as to where he was being led: the citadel.

The ancient city of the Indus Valley had been built in a style common to many of those of its period. A thriving city would surround a palace or fortress to which the inhabitants would retreat should they be under attack. In this area, normally on the highest point of the city, the well-to-dos of the city would reside in their ivory towers. As Richmond followed the orb up the incline to the wealthy part of town, he could not help but note, as he always did, how the construction of the buildings changed from those of the poor to those of the gentry and the nobility.

Eventually, they drew to a halt in a courtyard where the remains of a fountain dominated the centre of the space. The orb danced from side to side as it passed through an entrance to a building that Richmond knew exceedingly well. It was considered to be the dwelling place of royalty. Fashioned from fine, intricately carved bricks, the construction of the building was second to none. The orb darted into the building and drew to a halt by the remains of the far wall where it once more performed its little bobbing dance.

Richmond approached the curious entity, stood

and regarded the little ball of light. As he did, he could swear that he could hear something. Something faint.

It was like a song, a threefold rhythm that stroked the inside of his ears.

The orb bounced manically and started to throw itself against the wall.

Richmond just stood and watched.

The orb paused, spun around his head as it had before, down in the dig site, then resumed its pounding of the brick wall.

Richmond approached the orb and looked where it was assaulting the brickwork. He lifted his torch and swore as he noted that one of the bricks was a different colour from the others. It was slightly askew, as if it had been set differently and the ageing process had left it slightly discoloured. He reached into his jacket, pulled out a small trowel, and began to scrape around the edge of the masonry. The mortar came away with ease and, in a few minutes, the brick was wobbling in its socket. Using his fingers and the edge of the trowel, the archaeologist eased the small piece of masonry out of its resting place. He shone his torch into the dark recess and peered inside.

His eyes widened as he saw a wooden box concealed within.

Carefully, he reached in and pulled the box out. It was a very simple affair, plain but stout. There was no locking mechanism, just a length of cord tied around its middle and, attached to the fastening, a small steatite seal. Richmond held the torch between his teeth as he examined the seal.

The steatite seals of the Indus Valley were the mainstay of finds in the area. Marked with illustrations of figures both mundane and mythical, they were surmised to have been attached to wares as identifiers for trading. The problem was, they were all marked with a script which in the hundred years since its discovery, had never been fully deciphered. Popular motifs were water buffalo, wild animals, a horned god or priest and an enigmatic wo-man standing in a pipal tree. It was this latter image that adorned the exquisite piece of art in the archaeologist's hands.

However, it was different to all other representa-tions he had discovered of the goddess. Normally, she would be stood in her tree with the horned god chappie and others paying her homage. On this seal, she was sit-ting cradling a pair of infants.

Most unusual.

With great care, he rolled the cord to the edge of the box and slipped it off, pocketing the seal. He rested his hands on the lid of the box and turned his head to look for his glowing companion.

The small orb was nowhere to be seen.

In his head, the threefold tune grew louder and Richmond felt as if three repeating words were tickling at the edge of his senses.

He opened the box.

The creature stepped out into the night.

Well, that was fun.

As a human, he had always found the esteemed professor of archaeology somewhat up himself. Now… now that he had become what he truly was, it had been incredibly satisfying to put him in his place. To watch this ox of a man suddenly wither to nothing with no words to say had been majestic.

But that was not the end. No, appearing on the show was just the pretext to something greater.

The creature stretched his hand out in front of its face and smiled as its fingers drew together, coalescing into a long, sharp lance. It had been awoken to perform a simple task: destroy Richmond. It didn't know why, it just knew that was what it should do. Slowly, it stalked down the dark alley leading from the studio. Ahead, in the light of a flickering street lamp, it could see Richmond standing next to a large car as he smoked frantically on a rich-smelling cigar.

The creature allowed itself a smile as its mouth spread beyond the natural confines of its Van Dyke beard, further across its face than was possible for a hu-man, reaching literally from ear to ear.

It stepped forward, readying its attack, when it was aware of a light source behind it, casting its misshapen shadow on the footpath in front. The creature turned to face the intrusion, expecting to see someone fiddling with their mobile phone or a security guard with a torch check-ing that everyone had left the studio.

Instead, it was confronted with a small white orb that was bouncing up and down.

The creature frowned and batted at the ball of light with its misshapen hand. The orb just swept left and right, easily dodging the cumbersome blows.

The creature hissed in anger, its long dark tongue lolling out of its over-wide mouth. Dismissing the entity as a nuisance, it turned to resume its task at hand and star-ted to stalk down the alley toward Richmond.

"Now, I'm afraid we can't have you doing that, old chap."

The creature felt a firm hand descend onto its

shoulder, pulling it to a halt. It spun round to confront the owner of the hand and was met with a tall male human. He was long and thin, gangly of frame, under a practical grey suit. A pair of steel-rimmed spectacles framed a pair of bright, intelligent blue eyes.

"No, we can't have you do that at all," the man smiled kindly as the construct's world erupted into an explosion of pain.

"Willoughby? Is that you?"

Willoughby Chase, recently appointed personal assistant to Professor Robert Richmond casually dusted down his practical grey pinstripe suit, adjusted the steel-rimmed spectacles that framed his blue eyes and walked calmly out of the alleyway. "Just coming, Robert. I had a little matter to attend to."

"The final details for Castlerigg?"

"All taken care of."

Richmond nodded. "Best get going. You mind driving?"

Chase nodded and slipped into the driver's seat, allowing Richmond to sit in the back, alone with his thoughts. Thoughts of a single-minded daughter, a steatite seal of a mother with her twins and the contents of a certain box.

As he sped along the motorway towards the Richmond family home, Chase's non-human senses easily managed to concentrate on both the traffic and his employer's memories. He saw Richmond's hands opening a plain wooden box which contained the epitome of his life's work, a highly polished chalice that seemed to sing inside his head as he gazed into its reflective surface. But, even that was surpassed by the small, handwritten note that the professor had discovered tucked inside the bowl of the chalice. As traffic zoomed past, Chase saw the neatly written words on the ancient fragment of cloth as clear as Richmond had on the night when he had been led by his new personal assistant to the ancient Harappan palace:

"I love you, Daddy. Hope you like the family portrait. Elle."

Christmas Fear

"You want me to do *what*?"

I was standing on the deck of my pride and joy, *Icarus*, fastidiously removing any trace of smear or smudge from the brass safety rail when Suzi dropped the question. I turned and unkinked the knots in my back — annoying little signs of old age. Wretched things seemed to be growing even more numerous each passing winter than the tacky tinsel and lights with which other owners festooned their boats during this *festive* season. I placed my hands on my hips and stared at the young woman who was standing in front of me, fidgeting.

I've known Suzi Maloney since she was knee-high. Her mum and dad were old friends of mine from way back. Jack's been passed away some ten years now, so there's just Suzi and her mum. Plus, Kendra, Suzi's sweet little four-year-old bundle of energy and questions. You know the sort of stuff: "Why are you doing that? How fast can your boat go? Have you fought pirates? Have you got any liquorice?"

Not the sort of thing that her mum had just asked.

The dark-haired twenty-something was worrying at

the edge of the sleeve of her thick parka as I held her with my disapproving stare. I was hoping for an explanation. Instead, she just kept tugging away at a rogue thread that was trying to escape the frayed edge of her coat, her eyes studiously avoiding mine.

I eventually expelled a deep sigh, my warm breath fogging in the frigid air. "Suzi?"

This time she indeed looked up and my heart ached as I saw the desperation in her dark eyes. "I said that I need to hire *Icarus*. Buster has a very important business deal. He needs somewhere private to carry it out."

"I'll bet he does," I growled, and Suzi's eyes suddenly shot away again. "What is it this time? Timeshares on the Algarve? Holiday homes in Mull?" Those were the usual things that darling Buster was normally pushing. Suzi's latest paramour was one of those oily jerks who never quite stepped over the fine line of legality, but he certainly danced incredibly close, occasionally kicking a certain amount of sand on it to blur the edges. In the two months that he and Suzi had been dating, I had seen him leave a trail of disgruntled customers chewed up, spat out and empty of pocket with not a thing that they could do about it. He was certainly clever, I'd give him that, but he just stank of dishonesty and deceit.

I folded my arms and leaned against my freshly polished safety rail, the cold harbour water lapping down below against the side of my yacht. "Tell me," I asked, "why on earth do you go for these types? Is it the cars? The flash cash? Seriously, Suzi, didn't you learn when Kendra's dad skipped out on you when you were six months pregnant? Why can't you get yourself a *nice* lad?"

"Buster *is* a nice lad," she protested. "He looks after

me. With this deal, he says we'll be able to put thousands by for Kendra's uni fund. *Plus*, we'll be able to get her something sweet for Christmas, better than the usual tat that I can afford. Imagine the look on her face when she opens something worth having! Not like the battered second-hand garbage I got her last year."

I shook my head. It was the same old story: the boys would let their eyes wander over Suzi, and they would like what they had seen, so they would get at her through her kid. Promising Kendra the world was guaranteed to make her mother more pliable than a ball of potter's clay. "So, what's he planning this time? What luxury property is he selling off now?"

Suzi's young face suddenly brightened and she rummaged around in her handbag as Christmas shoppers wandered past on the quayside, chattering brightly about their seasonal purchases or other festive crap. "Oh, it's nothing like that," the young woman explained, handing over a cream envelope she pulled out of the bottomless depths of her ridiculously large handbag. "Buster's been able to sign a deal with a bank to let him sell bonds that they back."

Even before I opened the envelope, Suzi could not have failed to see the utter disbelief on my face. I ripped the envelope open and yanked the piece of paper out from inside. "What the hell is this?" I breathed as my eyes scanned the most godawful piece of fraud that I had ever lain eyes upon. "Seriously, Suzi, have you even *looked* at this?"

And there, finally, was the flicker of doubt. It crossed her eyes like a gull skimming the prow of *Icarus*: brief, but definitely noticeable.

I pressed home my advantage.

"Banks don't let other people sell their merchandise. They keep a very tight rein on those things. They're not going to want to share the profits."

"But Buster said..." Her voice drifted off.

"What? That it was a swell idea? That it would be the last scam he would have to pull?" I waved the A4 sheet in front of her. "Come on, Suzi. It's time to wake up. He's using you. You need to go to the police. There's no way he's doing anything *remotely* legal here."

Suzi chewed her bottom lip and my heart sank.

It was a habit that I had seen before from her many times when she was still a kid. Whenever she got caught doing something she knew to be wrong, her lip would get tugged and bitten as the guilt wormed away inside of her.

"Suzi, what is it?"

"Buster said that the bank needed an up-front payment to release the bonds into his business."

I groaned. "How much?"

"It... it was just fifty pounds. He said that it was a guarantee and would be paid back once we had sold the bonds for them. He said it was all above board."

I turned the letter over in my hand. The thick paper and the cream, embossed envelope felt expensive. Obviously, Buster hadn't wanted to stump up the cash himself this close to Christmas. Perhaps he was too busy saving up for a flash new car to park under his tree? "Did the money come directly from your bank account?"

She nodded.

There was no way that we could go to the police now.

"Okay, so this is what we do. We need to get him to back off. You tell him that everything should be fine here, but that I need to have a small chat with him over the fine details. Health and safety, you know? Can you do that, Sweetie?"

Another silent nod.

"Good girl. Get him back here tonight at six.

"I'll sort this for you."

I'll sort this for you.

Those were the last words that I ever heard my old man say.

When I was still a kid of single digits, my Nana, Dad's mum, lived with us. She was the oldest person that I knew. Her hair was pure white and incredibly thin, her skin wrinkled and she smelt funny. She stayed in bed all day, reading her bible and saying her rosary. I once asked her why she did this and she said that she had nothing else to do at her age, so she might as well make sure that she was right with God when he came for her.

Then, one winter, she fell ill. Seriously ill.

Her skin turned a pale grey and her jaw became slack, dribble running from the edge of her lips. She could hardly talk and my dad was obviously worried.

It was the day before Christmas and there had been a hell of a snowstorm the previous night. We lived out in the countryside, miles from nowhere. It was one of the perks of Dad being the senior partner in the town's largest legal practice. However, it meant that our nearest neighbour was only vaguely visible over on the next hill. The phone was out due to heavy snow having brought down the lines, so we could not call for a doctor or an ambulance. Dad decided that he had to go into town and get help for his mother, so he pulled on his warmest clothes and climbed the stairs to her bedroom. Bending over, kissing her softly on the forehead, he whispered the same words that I would say to a desperate young mother sixty years later.

Then he turned, left the house, drove off in the car and I never saw him again.

He was found dead in a frozen ditch the next day. Christmas Day.

Not only that, but an hour or so after he left the house, there was an almighty scream from Nana's room. Mum and I hurried up the stairs. I was smaller, faster, so I got there first. What I saw would haunt me for the rest of my life. The elderly woman who had been quietly making peace with her maker was sitting upright against the quilted headboard of the bed, her arm stretched out with her fingers splayed wide. Her dead face was set in a hor- rific, contorted scream of terror.

So, no, I'm not a big fan of the festive season. Whether it brings credit card debt or family anguish, Christmas sucks.

Six o'clock and Suzi arrived dead on the dot with dear old Buster. Suzi's latest is one of those who has a wide, insincere smile permanently fixed on his orange face. The guy is just awash with teeth, bronzer and ex- pensive cologne. Hell, it was almost Christmas and he looked like he was partying in Bermuda!

"Well, hi there, Harry!" he grinned, his snake eyes not once leaving me. "I believe you've agreed to host my little shindig."

I stroked my rough beard with my gnarled fingers. "About that. Not happening."

There was the slightest hint of surprise in the corner of his eyes, but that damned smile still did not flicker. "Oh? And why would that be? It'll be a great evening, so much fun."

"No, Buster," even saying the stupid name made me feel nauseous, "what *will* be fun is if you get all your shit together and just get the hell out of here. You're a fraud and this time you've gone too far. How dare you use Suzi like this?"

He chuckled to himself. "Well now, Harry, I don't see why I should follow you up on your *advice*."

"You know who I am. You know who my father was. People respect me; people who matter. You may be able to twist and manipulate the facts to keep you out of legal trouble, but I can make it so that life here is extremely un-comfortable for you."

There was a pause, then Buster took one step closer to me, his bright blue eyes fixed on my face. "Do you know what's uncomfortable, Harry? I'll tell you what's uncomfortable. Feeling me chowing down on your soul, that's what."

Well, this conversation had just taken an unexpec-ted twist.

Buster nodded. "Mmmm... yes, there we go. That sense of unexpected doubt and fear. Delicious. Now, for the last few years, I've been dining mainly on greed. Mod-ern society is so hard to scare these days, what with their precious internet and darling television. They just don't get me and my old kind anymore. No, but they get greed and, once it's been stoked up in them, I'll quite happily slurp away all that bitter brew.

"But fear... Now, fear is something else. It slips over the palate in waves: so sweet, so moist." His tongue slid across his thick lips. Lips which seemed more engorged than they had been just a moment ago. "Yesss... so sweet. It really hits the spot. Just like it did when I appeared to your dear old Nana. I walked up to the side of her bed and peered deep into her frail eyes. Do you know what she saw in mine?

"Nothing.

"All that reading. All those prayers as those stupid beads clicked away. All for nothing."

He licked his lips once more and this time there was no mistaking just how plump his fat lips had become. Moreover, his tongue had changed from pink to dark purple. It seemed to snake around his bright, white teeth.

Buster chuckled again, but this time it was more of a sibilant hiss. "Oh, yes. *There's* the good stuff. I can smell it all over you. You reek of it. It makes me so *hungry...*" And, with that, his tongue shot out of his mouth and lashed itself around my neck. I gagged and fell to my knees, my old hands trying desperately to unwrap the muscular noose, but it was wet and slippery so my fingers could gain no purchase. Buster continued to chuckle in his weird sibilant hiss. His eyes faded from blue to orange and I was aware of a green mist beginning to seep from his tanned skin.

I was also aware of Suzi behind him. She had reached into that abyssal handbag of hers and damn me for lying if she didn't draw out a knife. I couldn't tell what sort it was as my vision began to blur, but I could see the sharp blade glint against the twinkling fairy lights of the festively decorated quay.

I reached out towards her as she drew the weapon up and tried to cry out that this was not a good idea, but my words failed as the blade arced down into the meaty shoulder of boyfriend Buster, or whatever the hell he was.

There was a blinding flash and I was aware of a powerful force crumpling me down onto the deck as the tongue released its grip around my neck. I was also aware of a woman's scream and the sound of Suzi careering over the safety rail into the frigid wintry waters.

I forced my old body to take control of itself and dragged myself past where Buster had once stood. I hauled myself up against the railings and peered down into the black depths. I could not see her. She must have fallen like a stone and plummeted downwards, taking in water as she fell.

As my arthritic fingers fumbled to dial three nines on my mobile, I thought about a four-year-old daughter sitting at home waiting for her mother to return and I cursed Christmas even more.

Knocking at the Door

"If you have never done anything evil, you should not be worrying about devils knocking at your door."
Chinese Proverb.

"Sweetie, have you seen my cufflinks?"

"Which ones?"

"The blue ones. You know? The ones you bought me for Christmas last year?"

"You left them in the bathroom. Remember?"

Julian Hesketh frowned as he wandered out of the bedroom. Peering over the chipped and scuffed bannister, he called downstairs. "Which one?"

"Our one, of course." His wife of twelve years appeared down below. She smiled up from the long hallway that stretched from one end of their converted farmhouse to the other. Her youthful features were framed by the auburn hair that cascaded down onto her sapphire blue dress. In her arms, she juggled a colourful selection of discarded toys. "They're not likely to be in the kids' one are they?"

Julian nodded. "True. Sorry, I'm just rather scatty

tonight. What are you doing?"

"Having a quick tidy-up before we head out." A bright green plastic car slipped from her arms and clattered on the bare wooden floorboards. "Drat!" The immaculately attired woman bent to pick up the errant toy and the rest managed to tumble from her arms. "Oh no!"

"Angie, do you have to do that right now? We can get the kids to tidy up tomorrow."

The woman looked down at the mess of toys at her feet and sighed, absentmindedly tugging at a curled lock of hair. "No… No… I want to tidy up now."

Julian frowned and descended the creaking staircase. He walked over to his wife, who had bent down to collect the toys, put a warm hand on her arm and pulled her up. "What's wrong? Are you worried about tonight?"

Her blue eyes seemed to search his face. "Aren't you? It's such a big deal!"

"I know. I know. But it's for such a good cause, isn't it? Plus, it's a party and we *like* parties, don't we?"

"Well, yes… but ones that we've arranged. We've got no control over this at all."

"So, we just go with the flow and enjoy ourselves. It's not like we'll have any prep or cleaning up to do. We *are* the guests of honour."

"I know…"

"Well?"

"But we didn't do it for this, did we? You know? Raise all that cash. For *Kidsweek*."

Julian shook his head. "No, we didn't. But we can't snub the gratitude of others. That would be rude, wouldn't it?"

Angie glanced down at the scattered toys. "I know. I know. I suppose the tidying can wait."

"Indeed it can." Julian held out his crooked arm. "Now, why don't you help me locate these errant cufflinks, Mrs Hesketh?"

As they headed upstairs, smiling and chatting idly about the grand affair that was being held in their honour that evening, neither one of them noticed the dark shadow slip down the hallway below.

"The trick, Toby," the nine-year-old boy said to the attentive Cocker Spaniel, "is to be as quiet as possible."

The brown and white dog emitted a whispered "huff" as it flattened itself down on the threadbare carpet in mimicry of its human. Placing its muzzle on its large paws, like the boy, it peered intently under the sofa.

Zachary Hesketh nervously run his tongue over his upper lip as he adjusted his grip on the glass tumbler in his right hand and the sheet of card in his left. "They don't hear like we do," he explained to his canine companion. "They have hairs all over their legs which pick up vibrations and translate them into sounds. That makes them amazing predators.

"And incredibly hard to catch."

The boy's blue eyes peered out from under his unruly mop of fiery hair, studying the space beneath the long chair. They darted between dust bunnies, till receipts, lost change and random bottle tops. He closed his mouth and held his breath.

A long, spindly leg stretched out from behind an old, wrinkled crisp packet.

The boy started to smile.

There was a creak from the hallway as someone stood on one of the numerous loose floorboards.

The leg disappeared back behind the discarded

packet.

Zachary frowned. Typical. He wanted to look over his shoulder, but couldn't risk taking his eyes off the hiding place of the cardinal spider, so just ran through the logical suspects. Maia was outside kicking a football around in direct defiance of Mum's orders. Besides, she wouldn't have just made the floorboard creak. She would have bounced upon the wobbly flooring before leaping into the room and jumping on his back. It had to be Mum or Dad. Although he was sure he had heard them go upstairs just now. Perhaps Mum had resumed her tidying frenzy like she always did when she was stressed? It was weird she hadn't come in here and started fussing that he wasn't ready to go out to the party thing over in Morecambe.

The boy's train of thought was swept aside as the long, stripy leg re-emerged, this time followed by first two others, then five more. A wide grin spread across his freckled face as the body of the enormous arachnid crept into view. He once more adjusted his grip on the tumbler, feeling the weight in his hand, subconsciously tipping it back and forth in a trapping motion. Glancing quickly to his side, he reassured himself that Toby was motionless, the spaniel's obedient muzzle still resting on his paws.

Patiently, Zachary Hesketh waited as the cardinal spider skittered around the detritus under the sofa, before tentatively emerging into the early evening light of the living room. With one swift motion, the grinning youth swooped the tumbler over the spider and slipped the piece of card underneath, forming a perfect arachnid prison. He whooped with glee as he clambered up onto his knees and chuckled as Toby joined in the celebration by licking his face. The boy made sure to keep the card clasped tight under the tumbler as the spaniel expressed its excitement.

"It's a beauty, isn't it? Look at its colourings. Those stripes on its legs are gorgeous. Do you know why it's called a cardinal spider?"

Zachary took the dog's lack of response to mean that his furry companion had no idea.

"The story goes that Cardinal Wolsey kept finding loads of them at Hampton Court and he considered them to be lucky, so refused to let anyone squish them. It's a nice story, but it's probably just a myth."

"The thing with myths," came an unfamiliar voice from the doorway to the living room, "is that sometimes they turn out to be true."

Maia Hesketh was having the time of her life. She had already scored a hat trick that had secured her team's place in the FA Cup Final and was on the verge of blasting a penalty into the back of the net, her imaginary goalie standing quaking in front of her.

"The stadium holds its breath as Hesketh sizes up the task in front of her," she muttered to herself, pushing errant strands of wild auburn hair behind her ears as she paced backwards from the penalty spot. "They know just how much this goal will mean to her. Far more than some silly, fancy *gala* in poxy Morecambe." The eleven-year-old, auburn-haired girl reached her desired distance from the white football and paused, calculating in meticulous detail the angle and force she would need to kick it precisely into the top left corner of the small, battered plastic goal. "Yes, everything hangs on this last kick of the Final. Hesketh holds her breath, runs up to the spot… She shoots! She scores!!!"

As the football thunked into the back of the net, causing it to topple over, Maia sank down onto her knees, closed her eyes and saluted the early evening air with a double thump above her head. "Yes! Yes! Yes! Hesketh scores again."

However, her triumph was short-lived as, when she climbed to her feet, she bore witness to the huge muddy mark on the front of her blue dress. "Nonononono…" the girl wailed. Stupid dress! She had completely forgotten that she had been wearing it. Mum would go spare; she was stressed enough already, dashing around the house and tidying up random bits of stuff. Maia weighed up her options. The sensible thing would be to nip inside and scrub the dress down in the kitchen sink, but that ran the risk of being sprung by an over-wrought parent. Dad would be chill and tell her to grab another dress, but Mum… No, Mum had insisted that Maia wear this one so that they could wear matching outfits.

The young girl lifted up the filthy material. It wasn't too heavy. If she could sponge it down without Mum knowing, then she was sure it would dry out before they headed off. Her eyes scanned the overgrown garden for a solution to her predicament. As they came to rest on the summerhouse at the far end of the rough lawn, her mouth formed a grin. She hoicked up her dress and ran over to the family's pride and joy, or rather the green plastic water butt that harvested rainwater off its roof. Peering inside, she could see that it was almost full to the brim. Maia nodded, opened the door to the summerhouse and ventured inside, heading to a set of shelves at the far end. She loved coming out here. All the family did. Mum and Dad worked incredibly hard and weren't really into the whole domestic thing. Their house showed that. It was a ramshackle assortment of rooms that the farmer who had lived here before them had sort of thrown together. Mum and Dad kept saying that they would get around to modernising the place, but they just seemed to struggle to push it to the top of their to-do list, what with their jobs and all the charity work they did (hence the big, stupid gala thing tonight). So, they had bought the summerhouse. It had been built two years ago and was proving easier to maintain than the rambling pile in which they lived.

As a result, there was a cleaning kit kept handily on the shelf.

Maia grabbed the large yellow sponge from the ensemble of cleaning products and scurried back out to the water butt, desperate not to be seen. She soused the sponge in the chilled water and began to scrub at her messy front. At first, it looked as if nothing was happening, but after a few drenchings, the mud started to fall away from the fabric until it was once more its natural, if somewhat sodden, blue.

Maia nodded in satisfaction. She was sure it would dry out soon enough. Well, she certainly *hoped* it would.

It was as she was returning the sponge to the summerhouse's cleaning kit that she heard the terrified scream coming from the house.

Julian scooped his errant cufflinks off the marble surface of the vanity unit and began to fumble them into his shirt. Grimacing and grumbling under his breath as he did so, he considered how the world seemed obsessed with things being *just so*. People had to wear the right outfit for the right occasion. Diners had to drink the correct wine with the correct meal. Homeowners had to have a house that looked like it belonged on some daytime TV makeover show.

He shook his head as he slipped the second cufflink through its hole. This, he considered, was why the world was in the state that it was. People were so busy trying to live the damn dream, that they ended up turning their lives into a ruddy nightmare.

And it was inevitably the children that suffered.

Parents spent so much time working to pay insurmountable bills that their kids got no attention. Couples with money troubles constantly argued to the point that they split up and the children didn't know where they belonged. Single parents, destitute and despairing, turned to drugs and alcohol for respite from their godawful lives, meaning that their kids went neglected and malnourished.

This was why they had decided as a family to do all the work for *Kidsweek*. They had watched in horror last year as they'd seen stories of families who had lost everything and they had just sat in silence, looking at each other and their large family home. They had turned the television off and discussed what they could do to make a difference. They had planned, as a family, to all play to their strengths, from corporate functions to cake sales to sponsored walks, and they had spent the last year watching the cash roll in. To be perfectly honest, they had sort of taken their eye off the ball and hadn't fully realised just how much they had raised. It had only been when the representative from the charity had rung them a few weeks back that the enormity of their efforts had sunk in.

So, here they were, getting ready for a big shindig over at the Midland in their honour.

They hadn't expected anything like this. In fact, they had protested, saying that they were rather embarrassed about the attention. However, the woman from *Kidsweek* had insisted that it would be great publicity for the charity and would raise thousands, so they had quietly agreed to come along.

Not that they would stop their *own* fundraising. They considered themselves to be inordinately fortunate. They had food in their stomachs and a roof over their head, albeit a somewhat ramshackle one with a number of slates missing. Yes, they would have to get around to fixing up the house at some point, but there were more important things in life, weren't there?

It was, just like their fund-raising, a work in progress.

Julian's second cufflink clicked into place and he looked into the large mirror above the washbasin. Staring at the thirty-something man who was looking back at him, he smiled.

They were doing good.

That was when he heard the scream.

Angie sat on the edge of her marital bed and took a deep breath as she smoothed out the creases in her long blue dress. Why the hell had she chosen something so impractical to wear tonight? The damned thing looked glorious but it just wouldn't behave! The fabric seemed to crease every time she blinked, plus what if she spilt something down it? She was so damned clumsy and even more so when she was nervous.

Why the devil had they agreed to this?

Oh, she knew why. She did. It would raise more money for *Kidsweek*. Get all the local fat wallets in one place and empty them out into a big pot — they could afford it after all and should jolly well cough up. But that didn't mean that she was comfortable going along with the whole thing. She would be much happier curled up on the sofa with Julian, watching some trashy movie as the kids ploughed their way through a bumper bucket of popcorn and Toby snored quietly on his grubby old blanket.

This gala thing was just not her cup of tea.

She took a deep breath, imagined the rolling inside of her stomach settling down into a calm lake and stood up. *Needs must when the Devil drives*: that was the old saying wasn't it? Certain things just had to be done. Sacrifices had to be made. She'd made enough of those when she'd been studying for her accountancy exams. She'd burned the midnight oil, spurned all social activity and thrown herself into the world of dual-entry bookkeeping, spreadsheets, debits and credits. It had been dull, dull, dull, but ultimately worthwhile.

If it hadn't been for that course, she wouldn't have met her husband, given birth to her beautiful children and bought this weird assortment of rooms that were their family home. So, like that, tonight was a necessity. She would just have to suck it up and get on with it.

She gave the front of her dress a final, futile smoothing and headed out onto the landing.

Then she heard the scream.

Zach ran out of the living room, Toby barking on his heels. The man had been there. He definitely had. He hadn't imagined it. He knew it!

One minute, he had been holding a successfully captured cardinal spider, the next he had been staring at a man wearing a long black coat.

But then the man had just vanished.

"Zach? Zach? What's the matter?"

The boy glanced up the stairs as they creaked under the hurried footfalls of his parent.

"There was a man!" He pointed through the door to the living room. "In there!"

His mum frowned and turned to his father. "Jules?"

Julian strode across the hall and into the room. His eyes scanned around him and saw just the usual domestic mess: abandoned toys, open books, this morning's newspaper and a half-eaten slice of toast on a small plate. "No one here," he said, walking back out into the hallway.

"He vanished," the boy protested. "He was there, then he vanished."

"Sweetie," the boy's mother said, crouching down to his height, her dress flowing out around her. "People don't just vanish."

"Oh, I beg to differ," came a male voice from down the hallway.

They turned their heads as one and saw a dark-haired, sallow-faced man leaning against the wall. He wore a long black overcoat and was twisting his fingers in front of his face. Incredibly, sparks were bouncing off his fingertips. He clicked his fingers and, right in front of them, vanished into thin air.

There was an ominous creak from the staircase.

The Heskeths cried out as they watched the intruder slowly descend the stairs, more electricity building up between his fingers.

"Run!" Julian shouted and herded his wife and son down the corridor to the back door.

"Oh, please do!" called out the stranger. "I love that bit."

The back door flew open and Maia stood framed in

the dark from the outside. "What's…" she began, but her mouth snapped shut as she saw the rest of her family bolting towards her.

"Maia! Out!" her father screamed. "Out!"

The girl momentarily hesitated in stunned confusion, then did as commanded and backed out of the door. The rest of her family followed.

"Who… who is that?"

Julian shook his head as he looked up at his wife whilst doubled over, panting. "No idea. You don't recognise him?"

She shook her head. "What do we do?"

"You got your phone?"

"No. You?"

He patted his pockets then shook his head. "Kids?"

Maia pointed to the soaking wet dress. Zach looked back at the house. "Where's Toby?"

His parents made to say something, but before the words could leave their mouths, the boy was running back up the step of the house and yanking open the door.

"Zach!" his mother finally managed. "No!"

But it was too late, the boy had thrown open the door. They looked inside and saw the man just standing halfway down the hallway peering with a bored expression at the cocker spaniel that was barking maniacally at him.

"Toby!" Zach screamed. "Toby!" He made to rush in toward his beloved companion, but his father clasped a firm hand around his arm and pulled him back.

"Toby! Here!" Julian yelled out.

The dog cocked its head over its shoulder, saw its humans, turned and scampered down the hallway.

It got about three-quarters of the way before bolts

of lightning screeched out from the man's hand. They caught the spaniel in the middle of its back and sent it careening along the wooden floor, its paws sliding out to its sides and its blunt claws skittering on the plain boards.

Zach cried out and made to break free of his father as they watched the boy's best friend struggle to its feet and limp slowly along the hallway, the man in black slowly following behind. Julian placed a firm hand upon his son's chest and pulled him backwards, lifting the boy off his feet and into his father's arms.

As one, the Hesketh family edged backwards into the garden, unconsciously placing space between them and the intruder.

Another jolt of lightning illuminated the hallway of the house. It caught the unfortunate Toby full force and lifted him off the floor. The dog wailed in agony as its fur ignited from the elemental power. Walking forwards, the intruder grinned malevolently as he kept up the barrage of electricity on the household pet until one final shove with the lightning threw the dog's charred remains out of the house and onto the floor by the back step.

The parents clasped their children tight, trying to pull the eyes of the youngsters away from the dreadful scene. Maia mutely obeyed but Zach kept struggling to run to his furry friend, even after it was clearly apparent that Toby was no more.

"What do we do?" Julian breathed.

"The summerhouse," his wife replied and they manhandled their children across the grass to their pride and joy, running up the wooden steps and into the confines of the small wooden building. They slammed the door shut and stood panting in the stillness.

"What part of teleport do you people not understand?" came a familiar voice from behind them.

The Heskeths cried out as a unit, the parents pulling the children in even tighter.

The dark stranger was sitting in one of four old camping chairs that the family kept in the summerhouse. "Well, I suppose some people might call this *charming*," the intruder said, peering around the insides of the wooden building. "Personally, I think it's a bit of a dump. I mean, who in their right mind would want to spend time in a shed, of all places?"

"Who are you?" Angie asked, her hands running over the hair of her son. "What do you want?"

The camping chair creaked ominously as the man leaned back, crossing one leg nonchalantly over the other. "Who am I? Well, that depends on whom you ask, I guess. When you've been around as long as I have, you tend to accrue different names along the way. To some, I'm Ba'al. To others, Osiris. To thousands, I was a god-king. To a few, I was a destroyer of marriages. To me... I am someone who has been seriously wronged and all I want is what was taken from me."

"If... if it's about a donation you gave by mistake," Julian stammered, "just contact *Kidsweek*. I'm sure they can sort it out for you."

The man stared in obvious disbelief then shook his head. "You seriously think this is about some paltry little thing such as money? Did you not see how I barbecued your mutt back there?"

Angie felt Zach start to sob against her breast at the mention of his canine best friend. "Whatever it is you want, you didn't have to do that," she spat, ignoring the pounding of her heart.

The man looked down at his fingers, which were

crackling with energy. "No, you're right, I didn't have to do it. But I *wanted* to do it. And I always do what I want to." He flicked his wrist and a spark of electricity flew across the room, landing on the leg of the crying boy. Zach shrieked in agony and writhed in his mother's arms as he tried to run his hand down his leg. The dark stranger sat and chuckled. "Oh yes, I can do exactly what I want."

"You still haven't said what you want with us." Julian's mouth was dry and he felt his words sounded like crumpled paper.

"Ultimately, nothing. But for now, you will help me get something back that was stolen from me."

"Like I said, if it's about an incorrect donation…"

"Will you stop wittering on about your damned charity work?" the man roared, leaping to his feet, causing the chair to topple over. He reached out and a charge of lightning struck Julian on the right shoulder. The parent screamed in agony and surprise as he was catapulted backwards, his arms releasing his daughter as he did so. His wife, still trying to hold onto their crying son crawled over to her husband to check on him. He rolled over onto his side, rubbing his shoulder and managed a nod. They turned their attention back to the intruder and felt their stomachs lurch.

He was holding Maia, his fingers snaked through her hair. Flames burned brightly in his eyes. The girl's eyes, on the other hand, were screwed shut.

"Now, this is what's going to happen," the man snarled, his face contorted like a deadly animal. "You are going to stop asking stupid questions. Do you understand?" He flexed his hand and a shower of sparks ran down over the girl's scalp, causing her to shriek and fall to her knees. Her father made to reach for her. "Another step and she gets a fatal dose!"

Julian stopped dead in his tracks and nodded.

A second shower of sparks caused more scream-ing.

The girl's father didn't move a muscle. Just a solit-ary tear edged its way out of his left eye.

The intruder nodded. "Good. You understand your place, just like all you pathetic little lifeforms used to." He threw the sobbing girl back towards her family. Her father scooped up his child and cradled her in his arms. The stranger shook his head. "So weak. So pathetic. So easily manipulated. Why? Why did He create you? What was the reason?"

Through incomprehension and fear, the Heskeths were unable to provide an answer.

The intruder began to pace back and forth, continu-ing to talk about whatever it was that was on his mind. "He had no reason to make you? That's what I still don't un-derstand. It was pointless. A folly! Surely we were all He needed? We spent our whole existence, aeons of it, in His Realm, praising Him and adoring Him. Yet He wasn't sat-isfied. He craved more. More praise! More adoration! We weren't enough for Him. We were discarded like last sea-son's favourite toy. He craved something new and shiny.

"So, why shouldn't I? Why shouldn't I want what He wanted? Why shouldn't the toy want something itself to play with?" He paused and turned towards the cowering family. "That's all you are, all of you. Just playthings. No more than puppets whose strings are to be pulled for our amusement, making you hop and dance, fight and play. But eventually, the toys lose their shine. They become scuffed and tired. They may even want toys of their own, forgetting that all the time their actions have been the result of someone manipulating them, guiding them.

"Well, it's time that they were reminded of their place in all of this. It is time that the gods rise up and claim what is theirs. We shall jerk your strings and pull you into line, make you dance to our tune once again."

The man stopped and glowered at the Heskeths as he fished out a mobile phone. "What I need from you right now, though, is obedience and silence. I have to make a phone call."

Julian and Angie looked at each other as the dark man began a conversation on his mobile.

"Hello, Spallucci. Enjoying the festivities?" He picked up the fallen camping chair and resumed his seated position. "Well, let's see. The list is quite long, actually. I have had quite an inordinate amount of time on this spinning little ball of dirt to consider things. World domination; adoration from the masses; a really big gold throne. The usual. But right now, there's just one thing I want, and you know what that is. Something you stole from me!"

Julian Hesketh, chartered accountant, father and fundraiser, crouched in the corner of his beloved summer-house watching a complete lunatic having a phone conversation with someone whose name he did not recognise on a topic which he knew nothing about. In his arms, he held his sobbing daughter who loved to play football, climb trees and eat for England. Next to him was his wife, Angie Hesketh, chartered accountant, mother and fundraiser, crouched in a similar fashion, holding a crying son who was in pain and mourning the death of his best friend.

How had this happened?

Why was it happening?

They were good people. Things like this weren't supposed to happen to good people.

None of it made any sense.

They were completely powerless. The family that had raised thousands of pounds to improve the lives of children around the country were now in the middle of a dark, terrifying nightmare. They had to wake up soon, surely? This couldn't actually be real, could it?

He became aware of the intruder telling this Spallucci man their address. "Make sure you bring what is mine," he snapped, then hung up, before sliding his phone into a pocket of his long black coat.

"What will you do when he brings you your... thing?" Julian asked. "You'll go and leave us?"

The dark man raised both his hands and the summerhouse was filled with electricity and screams.

Maisie

"Well, all I'm saying is that I find the whole thing quite barbaric, that's all."

Five days in. Five days in and I'm seriously considering sacrificing this little prig to the guardians of the deep. However, Archibald Sullivan, captain of the cruise ship *Ephemera* had a well-honed sense of pragmatism. This meant that he was exceedingly adept in hiding any shred of annoyance caused by voyagers with too much money and not enough sense. So, when they brewed a typhoon in his head stronger than those his grandfather had steered through in the Indian Ocean, he just ran his callused fingers through the soft fur of the border collie that sat by his side at the dinner table and absorbed the calming vibes that seemed to flow from his ever-present companion.

Other guests were not so deft at avoiding the obvious bait for an argument.

"Well, I really don't see what the problem is, Mister Clee." Harrison was an ageing merchant banker and a regular passenger on Sullivan's trans-Pacific cruises. As a result, he was a regular face at the Captain's Table which meant that the observant seaman knew that now the touch paper had been lit, there would well and truly be fireworks of the most dramatic kind. "Let's face it, the beasts have a far nicer time of it on their cosy little farmsteads than they would in the wild. They get three square meals a day, fresh air and plenty of space in which they can wander and roam around without fear of predators. You put the poor things in a forest and they wouldn't last a minute."

"But that's only because we've engineered them that way over the millennia. We've selected the docile traits of animals that we've decided should be food and we've subsequently bred out any violence, any rebellion. They've not been subjected to the laws of natural selection. Darwin would have hated it!"

A snort of exasperation exploded from the other side of the table. "I bet Darwin enjoyed a good haunch of venison or fillet of beef," protested a chap by the name of Warren, whose expansive girth was threatening to expel the traumatised buttons of his tweed waistcoat. Sullivan seemed to recall he was something to do with astrophysics. Had a star named after him, apparently. "You're not telling me that, when he was aboard the *Beagle,* he lamented the fate of all the fish they'd have caught over the side?"

"Quite right!" It was apparently the turn of the other diner at the table to join in now. Jennifer Mills was a powerhouse of some renown in the boardroom, known for trampling over all who stood in her way as she rapidly carved her empire out of whatever it was that fools with disposable income decided was the latest greatest must-buy. Sullivan almost felt sorry for the poor lad. *Almost.* "Tell me, young man," she asked almost absentmindedly, as if it were of no real concern to her, whilst she meticulously sliced up her roast chicken breast into thin strips, "What do you think Darwin would have done should the *Beagle* have run aground? Do you think he could have lived off the sparse vegetation of some godforsaken desert island? Come to think of it," she paused, her intense blue eyes peering across the table, "What would *you* do? Would you eat sand? I believe it plays havoc with one's fillings."

The young man lay down his knife and fork and seemed to ponder this question for a short while before answering. "I would stick to my principles. It is ethically wrong to eat meat, no matter what the situation. I would find a way to survive that did not involve cruelty. There would *have* to be something edible there. I would just use my ingenuity and intelligence to locate and prepare it."

Mills' blue eyes held the young man for a short, uncomfortable moment before shaking her head and returning to her roast chicken, obviously deciding that the banal argument wasn't worth letting her delicious food go cold.

The other diners, however, were not of the same opinion. So it was that the argument continued, round and round. Sullivan just sat quietly in his seat, letting the increasingly heated discussion drift over him, insensitive to the words, unwilling to intervene, knowing that whatever he said would be considered wrong by one side or the other. So, he just sat and let the young fool talk himself into circles, spurting half-hashed arguments as to why the whole world should be following a vegan diet. Instead, Sullivan sat and stroked the soft fur of his canine companion who had affectionately positioned her head on his lap, her brown eyes staring up at him.

It was as he was gazing down at those deep brown,

calming eyes that Sullivan became aware that someone had spoken his name.

He groaned internally.

"I beg your pardon? I was miles away."

"I asked," said Clee, "do you not feel it is cruel keeping your dog on a ship? Surely she would be happier running around the fields at home?"

Sullivan visibly sighed. He hadn't wanted to get involved; it wasn't his place as host. However, when some little snot dared to criticise his attachment to his dog... Well, that was just too much.

The captain noticed the regular passengers shrink back somewhat in their seats.

"Let me explain something about Maisie here, young lad. I didn't pick her up from some dirty little puppy farm back home. I didn't pay a packet to some knavish farmer who had her mother shackled up as a pathetic breeding machine once she'd hurt her leg whilst out herding sheep. I didn't even purchase her from some bored middle-class housewife who had a little hobby on the side that produced cute bundles of fur that helped to pay for her jolly off around Gran Canaria with her illicit toy boy once a year. No, Maisie here, chose me. We were docked in the Philippines three years ago and I had gone ashore to check on the buying of supplies from this local chap I know. When I came back, blowed if I didn't find a border collie asleep in my cabin. To this day I haven't the foggiest as to where she came from or how she got there. She must have nipped on board when no one was looking and somehow managed to scrabble her way in past my door. Collies are incredibly smart dogs, so I can see her having managed it. I asked around the crew and passengers, but no one knew anything and she seemed quite happy where she was. So, when we sailed away, she accompanied us. And she has been part of my crew, part of my *family* ever since.

"You ask whether she would prefer fields and the such to run around in. Have you taken the time to watch her interact with those around her? Have you seen the joy she gets from sitting, spending time with crew and passengers, intently watching them as if she is studying them, trying to discern what it is they are doing or what it is that they are talking about? No, I guess you haven't, because you sir are a self-righteous imbecile who has latched onto the latest in a long line of fashionable ideas prevalent in the overindulged middle-class society, which you spout at a dinner table to make yourself look important whilst blind to the fact that you are actually insulting all those around you with your half-baked, poorly considered ideas. Ideas of which, quite frankly, I have had a full stomach. If you will all excuse me, I shall take my leave."

Captain Sullivan arose from the table, threw his napkin down on his half-eaten plate of food and stalked out of the room. Maisie watched him leave before gazing her eyes around the remaining diners, lingering slightly longer on the cause of all the fuss. She then turned and padded out of the room, following her beloved companion.

The storm came out of nowhere and struck, as all horrific things do, in the middle of the night. The events that followed the monstrous waves cracking the *Ephemera* in two were a complete blur for Clee, but somehow he found himself adrift alone in the ocean in a small lifeboat. Opening his eyes, he winced as a sharp dagger lanced his right temple. Upon inspecting the source of the pain, his hand came away covered in blood and his rocking, swaying world of dark skies greyed out.

He was next awoken by the sensation that he was no longer moving. Opening his eyes once more, slower this time, with greater care, he saw the sun beating down upon him. He stretched his lips in order to speak, but only managed a faint squeak. Gently touching his head, he determined that the cut had healed over and he gingerly rolled over. The lifeboat neither rocked nor swayed.

Easing himself to the edge, he discovered that the boat had been washed ashore on a small beach. The beach belonged to a tiny island that appeared to be no larger than a suburban house, in the middle of which grew a green stand of undergrowth comprising a few trees, some sparse shrubbery and patchy fronds of grass.

Clee crawled out of the boat and dragged it completely onto the shore, pulling it as best he could above what appeared to be the tideline. After this energy-sapping task, he paused, gathered his strength and leaned on the side of the boat to prevent the world around him from spinning. When he could tell once more which way was up, he proceeded to unfasten the survival kit from its secure location under a seat in the boat. Unsnapping the box, he rummaged under a foil blanket and dug out the food rations. They came in simple foil packaging upon which there were no markings save their calorific value. Clee frowned and ripped one open, gave the contents a sniff and frowned. His stomach roared but his brain protested.

What the hell was this stuff? How could he trust it was suitable for him?

Placing the food rations down on the shore, he reached into the boat and extracted an axe, then turned to eye up the trees in the centre of the island.

In a few hours' time, the castaway had a reasonable fire burning bright and he had dug up some roots from the plant life on the island.

After another hour he had cooked them in some of the water supplies from the raft.

Then, after just five, agonising minutes, the entire contents of his stomach had been purged from both ends of his body.

Clee passed out as far away from his expelled filth as possible.

Two days later and he felt strong enough to try to eat again. Swallowing down his moral views, he returned to where he had left the discarded ration packs. All that remained on the sand was a wet puddle. Clee knelt and stared helplessly at the place where the hungry sea had snatched away his only form of sustenance and would have wept, had his body been hydrated enough to do so.

He lifted his head up on his weak shoulder muscles and stared pathetically out at the monstrous sea, the cruel sun beating down upon his blistering skin. As he gawped out into the void with no particular plan of survival coming to mind, he became aware of a black dot forming in his field of vision some miles out. Having nothing else to do, he just stayed kneeling where he was, gazing at the black spot as it approached, growing in size until it came to resemble a black and white dog standing on a floating piece of ship's hull.

All Clee could do was frown in bewilderment as the piece of flotsam bumped up onto the shore and Maisie the border collie hopped nimbly off onto the beach.

His bewilderment increased tenfold when the dog padded over to him and said, "Well, that was a close call.

Are you okay?"

Clee's mouth just flapped open and shut as he tried to make sense of the situation.

"Looks like you took quite a bump there, buddy," continued the dog, its muzzle motioning to Clee's temple. "Why don't I take a look at that for you?"

Clee answered with a distinct rumbling from his stomach. The last remnant of liquid in his mouth began to coat his tongue and he swallowed, ignoring the dry pain in his throat. He threw himself in a clumsy, knotted-leg fashion up the beach to where he had left the axe. Grabbing it with trembling hands he turned around and advanced on the dog.

Maisie frantically shook her head. "Now, come on. Calm down, buddy. There's no need for this. It's really not a good idea. Trust me, help is on its way. It'll be here in just a few hours, tomorrow at the latest."

But the poor dog's protests were in vain as the axe swung in its deadly arc.

The next morning, Clee awoke to the most unsettling of sensations. At first, he thought that he had not cooked the flesh of the animal correctly, being somewhat out of practice. However, when he had ascertained that he wasn't going to be sick, he sat up and gazed at his hands.

But they weren't his hands, were they?

They had to be, they were the hands that he'd always possessed, the ones he'd been born with. Four fingers and a thumb on each. He raised them up and ran them through his wet, knotted hair. Hair that he had also possessed for a considerable time now, but felt curiously alien.

"I did tell you not to do that," came the voice of Maisie.

Clee's head spun around, frantically trying to locate the ghost of the dead canine.

Clee's own lips moved as the voice that wasn't his just sighed.

Clee's vision started to blur. Everything took on a light red hue.

His lips moved once again of their own volition. "All you can do is just sit back and let this happen now, I'm afraid."

Clee watched as his diminishing senses seemed to curl into a small, black circle before dissolving into nothing.

Daniel Clee, ardent vegan, slayer of dogs, ceased to exist.

The creature that had been inside the body of the dog and that now inhabited the body of Clee stood and stretched its new arms. As it did so, a shining sphere a metre or so in diameter descended from the sky and settled on the shore. A door slid open from its surface and two gaseous forms drifted out onto the island.

"Hi, guys," the creature in the form of a human greeted them. "What took you so long?"

They explained in his head that they'd been held up and asked how his observations had gone.

"Bit of a bust, really," it shrugged. "Some pockets of compassion but, on the whole, far too argumentative and violent. Shall we head off?" Its true gaseous form extracted itself from the pores of the dead human host, which it left discarded on the beach, then drifted into the capsule with its kindred and shot off into the heavens, never to be seen again.

Date Night

That was a great evening. I really enjoyed it.

You did too? Cool.

Yeah, the waiter was a bit odd, wasn't he? I mean, what was the deal with his eye? He was all, you know, *Columbo.* When we placed the order, I expected him to go, "Oh, just one more thing..."

Yeah, weird. But the food was nice, wasn't it? Especially the steak.

I know, it was gorgeous. So tender. And as for that chocolate thing...

Me too. I could definitely have eaten double. I would have to do twice as much work at the gym tomorrow, though.

Sure do. Regular routine every day. Twenty minutes on the treadmill, some free weights then fifteen minutes on the cross-trainer. I find it wakes me up in the morning.

Ha ha! Thank you. It's more of a fitness thing. My job's completely sedentary so the exercise stops me from piling on the pounds.

That's right, at the town hall. I see you've been paying attention; I like that. It's a dull job but, in this so-called paperless society, there are still reams of processed trees and someone has to file them all away correctly.

Interesting? No way! It's dull, dull, dull. Believe me. Day after day, walking into the same grey office and discovering more and more of the same buff-coloured folders piled high on a desk you only just cleared the night before. It's like the film. You know? *Groundhog Day*?

Seriously? You've not seen it? Bill Murray's in it. The guy from the original *Ghostbusters*.

That's right, the one who was cheating on the psych tests at the beginning of the film. I think he was the voice of *Garfield* too. Anyway, in *Groundhog Day*, he has to live the same day over and over again until he does something to break the spell, so to speak, and let his life continue. It almost drives him mad. Sometimes my job can be a bit like that. It does my head in.

Well, it's a job isn't it and it's not like there's a mass of them out there. Certainly not ones that pay as well.

I'm sorry. I really am. I'm rambling.

No, no. It's okay. It's just... Never mind. We've had a great time, haven't we?

I know. I was blown away when you answered my request on *Date Me*. I'd been on there for ages and had no real luck whatsoever. I mean, I dated some girls, but they weren't really my type.

Ha ha! Yes, perhaps it *was* fate. You never know, do you? Well, look, here's my place.

Early? Well, I suppose it is. Listen... How about... Not being, you know, *weird* or anything... But do you fancy a nightcap?

Okay. Cool. Come on in, then. I'll warn you though, I'm not the tidiest of guys. Dusting's not my forte. Living room's just through here.

Thank you. I try my best. I'll just go get those drinks. Scotch?

Ice?

Okay. It's a single malt. I prefer those to blends.

Yeah, that's right. Classier. Here you go.

You like?

Yeah, very peaty. I think it's something to do with the distillation process. I'm not too sure. I just know I like it.

Oh! Oh... Oh, well... I wasn't expecting *that*.

No, no, it's fine. *Really* fine. I like you too. Can't you tell by the way that I'm grinning my head off here? Wow! I just wasn't expecting that. I mean, it's not as if I'm much of a catch — just a clerical guy in a dead-end job. Listen, wanna see something special?

Okay. It's downstairs. I think it would suit you.

Intrigued? Cool. Come on then. Mind the top step. It's a bit steep.

Yeah, sorry it's so dark. I'll just grab the light switch.

That's right, they're under the sheets. Go on, lift one.

A shop dummy? Ha ha! No, silly. Look here, at the others.

That's right. They're real. I stuffed them myself.

What? Oh. Oh, dear. Well, I thought you might...

Well, there's no need for that! Get back here!

No. No, I won't let go. You play all coy all evening and toy with my affections then ask to come back here to seduce me, you slut. You're just the same as all the others, time and time again.

Stop that!

I said, "Stop that!"

Don't wriggle, you'll bruise. They're so hard to get out. There. That's it. Shhhh… That's it. Calm now. Quiet. Good girl. That's better.

That's better.

Family Reunion

Things aren't going as planned, decided Dave Nichols, former comic book store owner, now a night-dwelling vampire. He surmised that this really ought to be his motto these days. *Perhaps,* he thought to himself as he stood before the imposing gothic church in the small East Midlands market town, *I ought to find out the Latin translation?* "I could have it engraved on my coat of arms," he mumbled to himself.

"Have *what* engraved upon your coat of arms?" The redheaded woman turned around from the lock of the large wooden door in which she was manipulating numerous metal rods. Her bright green eyes twinkled in the night air.

"Things aren't going as planned," he said. "I was wondering what it was in Latin."

"Do they ever?" she grunted as she rooted around inside the huge, wrought iron, mediaeval lock, twisting and turning a long, crooked implement she had just selected from an old cloth satchel at her feet.

Dave shrugged. "It could sit nicely under my personal animal."

"Oh? And what would that be? Damn it!"

The male vampire sat down on the cold stone steps leading up to the south door of the church, not that he really felt the cold these days. He was just sort of aware of it. He looked glumly out across the rows of deserted market stalls. "I'm not sure. Perhaps a griffin? They look cool. It could be a *griffin rampant*. You know, upright with its claws extended."

"As long as it's not a sodding dragon," Tigress rumbled.

Dave nodded in agreement. Definitely not a dragon. "How's the breaking and entering coming along?" he asked over his shoulder, already knowing the answer from the ancient curses that his colleague was chuntering under her breath.

"Let's just say that they knew how to make a decent lock back in the day."

Dave rubbed a hand over the back of his neck. He wasn't supposed to get easily tired or fatigued but the drive down here had taken it out of him both physically and emotionally. The smallest passenger in the car had talked continually, even more than the garrulous Tigress. Four hours of constant questioning.

"Will I like it?

"Are we nearly there?

"Have you been there before?

"Can I play with my toys?

"How fast are we going?

"What was Troy like?

"Are we nearly there?

"Has your hair always been short?

"Do you have any sweeties?

"Why are you grinding your teeth?

"Are we nearly there?"

The Child of Cain shuddered. "They probably had more things that were actually worth stealing back then."

Tigress gave the door an angry kick, causing it to shudder slightly in its frame. The redhead muttered one more obscenity as she thrust her assortment of apparently useless tools into her satchel. Scooping the old bag off the stone floor and slinging it over her shoulder, she came and slumped down next to the male vampire. "What, mediaeval high definition wide screen TVs?"

He ignored the sarcasm. "You know that's not what I mean; you lived through it. Think about all the gold and silver in these places. If it was stolen, it could be melted down before anyone noticed. Things must have been easier to fence back then." He paused. "Did they *have* fences back then?"

The female vampire shoved her hands into the pockets of her russet-coloured leather jacket and stretched her legs out in front of her down the steps. "There was this guy Scorp and I met once in this godawful village somewhere in the arse end of Burgundy. Can't remember his name. All I can recall was how bad he stank. Jesus! We seriously had him pegged for a construct, so we did the usual and stalked him for a while to check him out. Turned out, he was just very unsanitary. Mind you," she mused, "back then, most of them were. Anyway, he was known as the local guy to go to should you require something a bit unusual, shall we say? The thing was, the local authorities knew this too and they were constantly trying to catch him out whilst he was playing his little game. But, gods he was a sly one. Whenever there was the slightest whiff of a sheriff's man, his shabby little cottage turned from an Aladdin's den of purloined treasures into, well, a shabby little cottage. Don't ask me how he did it. We never worked it out."

"What happened to him?"

"Plague. Plague happened to everyone back then."

Their heads turned in unison to look along the path that curled along the edge of the parish church. They heard Tigress' partner, Scorpion, approaching before they saw her. Technically, they heard her diminutive companion rather than the mute vampire.

"And when I see my mummy, I'm going to give her a big hug. I'll tell her about all my adventures. I'll tell her about all the things I've seen, all the fun I've had and… and… all the people I've killed."

As the blonde vampire came into view she wore a drawn face which shouted, "Please, impale me now!"

"And people complain that *I* talk too much," Tigress grinned. "Hey, Scorp! You had any luck?"

The silent vampire shook her head.

"No joy? Ah well, at least you had company."

Scorpion may never have spoken much but her face was exceedingly adept in expressing her emotions, as it was right now.

Tigress held up her hand in apology. "Hey, just joking." She looked down at the small entity that resembled an eight-year-old girl, albeit an eight-year-old girl from your crazed acid trip nightmares. The child was wearing a flowing white dress, over the shoulders of which cascaded long green hair. From her face blazed two emerald orbs that were meant to be eyes. "So, short stuff, you excited then?"

The weirdling practically bounced up and down on her bare feet as she clapped her hands together in glee. "Oh yes, oh yes! Have you opened the door yet? I can't wait! I can't wait!"

"I'm afraid we're having problems in that department," Dave apologised. "The lock is proving somewhat problematic."

"Like I said when we arrived," Tigress commented, eyeing up the stout oak door, "I could just kick it in."

Dave shook his head. "No. Nightingale said we had to be in and out with as little fuss as possible. No one must know that we've brought the Potency here."

The three vampires looked down at the weird resemblance of the small girl.

"Because of course, no passerby would ever notice a small girl with green hair and glowing eyes..." Tigress noted.

"It's four in the morning in February. The only passersby will probably have seen worse due to what they've been imbibing or smoking." The male vampire walked up to the door and rattled the resolutely unbreakable lock. "You didn't find any other way in?" he asked Scorpion.

She shook her head once more.

The three vampires stared sullenly at the locked door, wishing it was open, wishing they were far away from this place.

"I can open it," came a small voice.

Three sets of eyes turned to look at the human manifestation of a green homicidal rock that had been fashioned at the dawn of creation.

The small girl skipped down the stone steps and into the churchyard. Her shining green eyes searched around for a suitable spot, which she located in a dormant flower bed. She held out her hand and the vampires watched in morbid fascination as the wet soil began to move below her dancing fingers. It drifted lazily up into the air, eddying and spinning together as it did so, coalescing into a dark ball. The Potency's emerald eyes blazed as she guided the ball of clay over to the path in front of the church, where it lengthened out and expanded until it stood like a pillar that measured over two metres tall. The weirdling child spread her arms to her sides and, as she did so, arms emerged from the column of clay, mirroring her movements. Next, it split at its base, fashioning a pair of solid legs. Finally, as the child grinned in glee at her deadly creation, a wide mouth split across the crude dome that rose up from the creature's broad shoulders. A black tongue whipped out from the gash in its face and flickered left to right, scenting the night air.

The construct levelled its visage towards the three vampires, uttered a wet, deathlike resemblance of a growl and stretched out its arms, a pair of wicked-looking lances forming at their ends.

The Potency squealed in delight as her brand-new killing machine stalked across the churchyard toward the vampires. Vampires who were now trapped in the south porch of the mediaeval church.

"Quae non iens ut cogitavit!" Tigress growled, flashing her sharp incisors.

Dave shot her a confused look as he braced himself for the attack.

"Things aren't going as planned," she explained, "but in Latin."

When a vampire is born and becomes one of the Children of Cain, a direct descendant of the murderous brother from the biblical book of Genesis, they are told three truths that they must always remember: Find the Eternals. Protect the Twins. Await the Divergence. These are the three tenets to which every vampire knows they must adhere. They are their *raison d'être*. They are the purposes for which they were created.

There is, however, one other unwritten rule that they all instinctively follow.

If you see a construct, you kill it before it kills you.

Three vampires standing in the south porch of a church in a small market town in the East Midlands of the United Kingdom were currently assessing their situation with precise rapidity. They had been sent to reunite a strange little entity with its mother, a sentient river that flowed around Creation, separating Heaven, the Physical Realm and Beyond. However, they were now faced with one of the universe's ultimate killing machines. This clay-based golem had just been conjured out of the ground by their aforementioned ward whilst the excited little weird-ling eagerly awaited its family reunion. Not only this but the three Children of Cain were trapped up against a solid oak door that remained defiantly locked.

Going through their minds were the following:

Dave Nichols (former owner of a comic book store in Lancaster, born a vampire when hit by a car in the car park of a local comic convention), *Can I get around its back? Is there enough room?*

Tigress (oldest living vampire, born to her current life at the birth of the Bronze Age after what turned out to be a somewhat fatal hunting accident), *When I get my hands on that child's neck I'm going to squeeze so very, very hard...*

Scorpion (mute partner of Tigress, born a vampire in the fiery ruins of Troy after predicting her city's fate), *Here we go again...*

The two female Children of Cain had fought side by

side countless times over the past two millennia and knew each other's tactics as if they were their own. They were notorious for their brutal efficiency in the despatching of constructs, hunting them down with the same glee as a lepidopterist chasing through a verdant meadow after a red admiral that dances on a summer breeze. They were a pair of gauntlets fashioned for a single task — the eradication of the creatures that one day would rise up and serve Kanor, the individual from the future that would decimate humanity.

The male vampire, by comparison, was relatively new to the job. When it came to battle strategy he was more versed in theories regarding the final conflict in Marvel's *Endgame* and could explain in intricate detail how the whole plot was flawed because the forces of good actually had an overpowered weapon in their hands in the form of Captain Marvel whom they hardly used, instead sacrificing hundreds of pawns to the forces of Thanos. Plus, it was nothing like the comic.

So, throwing someone who complained about fictional wars on Blu-Ray in with two hardened warriors who had witnessed some of the greatest battles in history was always going to be a disaster should it ever come to pass that they needed to fight for their lives.

Tigress and Scorpion immediately launched themselves upwards, running up the stone walls of the porch and vaulting themselves behind opposite shoulders of the construct. They would have landed lightly on their feet and would have struck with deadly efficiency at the golem, had Dave not darted around its side, placing himself in the exact spot where Tigress had aimed to land. The redheaded vampire swore loudly in an ancient tongue as the two of them clattered to the floor. Scorpion darted to their aid and lifted them quickly to their feet.

The three spun to stare at the construct, expecting it to bear down on them, painfully skewering the three of them in the process.

Imagine their amazement as they watched it, instead, thump its way forward a few steps to the door of the church. Extending one of its arms, it slid the lance up to the lock. The malleable material of which the limb was composed rippled and slipped with easy fluidity into the lock before setting once more into a firm solid. The construct twisted its wrist and there was a loud click from the mediaeval security mechanism.

The golem retracted its arm and turned to face back out of the porch, awaiting further instructions.

"Isn't it clever?" the small manifestation of the Potency cooed as she bounced up the porch steps, throwing herself around one of the creature's trunk-like legs. "I do love my toys." She gave a quick worried look at the vampires. "It's not here to kill anyone. I made a promise. You won't tell, will you?"

The three vampires just stared at each other before Dave shrugged, walked over to the door and turned the large iron handle. The huge portal that was more accustomed to welcoming worshipping parishioners than three stealthy vampires, a manifestation of a primordial entity and a mindless clay killing machine, swung inwards with ease. A pleasing aroma of old incense enticed the enhanced senses of the male vampire as he turned to talk to the Potency who was lovingly stroking her clay giant. "Thank you for that, but perhaps it would have been a good idea to warn us?"

The weirdling harrumphed and patted the construct on the tip of one of its sharp lances. It slipped its arms out and scooped her up, cradling her in its embrace. The three vampires just shook their heads in unison and entered the church.

The first thing that struck them was the pews. There were lots of them, all old, dark wood rather than the utilitarian chairs that seemed to be more in vogue in modern churches. Tigress ran her fingers along the back of one as they walked quietly, reverentially, towards the centre of the church, to the main aisle. "They definitely made sure things would last back then," she whispered in an awed fascination. "These are beautiful. So smooth." She glanced up to her right, in the direction that the pews faced and paused, letting out a low whistle. "Amazing," she breathed as her eyes took in the rood screen that crossed in front of the chancel. Atop the wooden structure stood an intricate, life-size representation of the crucifixion. Jesus hung upon the cross with his mother on one side and his Beloved Disciple on the other. A visage of perfect serenity was carved into the face of the dying messiah. "Perfection," she whispered.

She felt a cold set of fingers slip into her hand and turned to see the smiling face of Scorpion. "It's okay, Babe. I'm not getting maudlin."

The blonde vampire rose an eyebrow.

"Well, okay. Just a bit."

Scorpion lent across and kissed her life partner softly on the cheek.

"You guys okay?"

The two females nodded. "Yeah," Tigress explained as she gazed back up at the crucifixion screen. "It's just that we knew the guy that carved," she waved a hand around, taking in the old woodwork of the rood screen and the crucifix, "this."

Dave nodded. "Yes, you mentioned him back in Lancaster, when we met Spud, the grotesque. The same craftsman carved him as well, didn't he? Constructs killed him."

Tigress' face darkened as she looked across the vampire's shoulder to the gigantic clay golem that was standing cradling the weirdling in its arms. "They kill everything that is beautiful," she hissed.

A solemn silence fell across the three.

Eventually, Dave said, "Right, we'd better get on with what we came here to do." He turned to make towards the stone font at the west end of the nave but paused in his steps when an ominous crunching noise came from over his shoulder. He turned to see Tigress forcing the lock on a wooden door in the rood screen that led to a small side chapel. "What the hell are you doing?" he cried.

"What *I* came here to do," she explained as she pushed the door inwards, its brass lock falling uselessly to the floor. "You think I give two hoots about that crazed piece of rock and its *toys*?" She spat the final word with extreme malignancy before entering the chapel, her eyes scanning around and about. "Not a chance. I've come for something that's *ours*. Something that was given to us and was stolen away."

Dave looked to Scorpion for support and explanation, but the mute vampire just shrugged and followed after her partner.

"This looks like a lady chapel," Tigress muttered under her breath. "It's got to be here somewhere." She stalked down into the middle of the small side chapel and paused, her hands on her hips, as she cast her heightened eyesight around about her like a predator searching for its prey that it knows instinctively is hiding in the undergrowth. "Where else would they put it?" she asked, part to herself, part to Scorpion, who was now standing beside her. "It's *got* to be here."

Dave dithered for a moment in the nave of the church, trying to decide what he should do. Nightingale had been very clear on the matter. "Get in. Stow the Potency as close as you can to the font. (I remember there being a loose flagstone. You can use that.) Get out. Nothing else."

This, however, was definitely veering into the realm of *nothing else.*

He checked on the Potency. She was happily playing pat-a-cake with her construct. He shook his head and chased after the other vampires. "What is it you're looking for exactly?" he asked.

"Do you not listen?" Tigress called over her shoulder as she abandoned her search in the lady chapel and progressed into the chancel. "I told you this when we were back in Lancaster. A small wooden Madonna and Child. Nathan carved it for us but the damned construct who killed him took it and brought it here. Our little leader saw it when she was here as a mortal." She stomped up and down between the choir pews, inspecting every available ledge or shelf where one could stand a small statue. "What the hell have they done with it? Anything up there?" she called to Scorpion who was now busy hunting around behind the high altar. The blonde shook her head.

Dave sighed. *In for a penny in for a pound*: he thought to himself. "Perhaps it's in the vestry?" he suggested, nodding to a small wooden door that led off the sanctuary to the side of the altar.

Tigress nodded absentmindedly. "Worth a try."

The three passed through the oak door into the small room where the priest would prepare for the service. Wardrobes and cupboards lined the walls and a large cope chest dominated the space under a small, leaded window.

Upon the stone windowsill sat a perfectly carved wooden statuette of a Madonna and Child.

It was very rare that Dave witnessed the verbose Tigress as quiet as her long-suffering partner, but this was one of those occasions. The normally fiery redhead just stood in front of the cope chest, her pale hands up in front of her mouth, which was open in a mixture of surprise and relief. Red tears tracked down her cheeks.

Scorpion leant over the chest and carefully picked up the figurine before bringing it over to her companion.

"It's just as exquisite as I remember," Tigress breathed, carefully tracing the statuette's delicate working with a tender finger before carefully stowing it amongst the assortment of lock-picking tools in her cloth satchel.

Scorpion gently hugged the shoulders of her partner, then looked up at Dave and smiled.

The male vampire nodded. "Okay. Now we have a job to do, don't we?"

"Yeah," Tigress whispered, her voice hoarse with emotion. "Let's hide that damned rock and get out of here."

"So, what, we just slip it under a loose flagstone and skedaddle?"

Dave stood staring at the stone font in front of him.

Five words stood staring back.

Knaves Are Not Our Responsibility.

"I asked, are we just to..." Tigress paused. "Hey,

you okay?"

The male vampire performed the representation of a deep breath, a reflexive remnant of his mortal life, his lungs no longer requiring air. That font. The damned font. He turned around and gazed up at the wooden figurine that was crucified above the nave and nodded. It was the right place, in decidedly better condition, but definitely the right place. He ignored Tigress and, instead, said to Scorpion, "You recognise this place?"

The mute solemnly nodded.

"Okay," Tigress' voice was unusually low, worried. "What am I missing here?"

Dave performed another mock breath and turned to her. "I saw this place in my birth dream. This is where I will die. At the hands of Kanor, himself."

The redhead swore under her breath, then asked her partner, "You knew this?"

Scorpion shook her head.

"Then why that fancy little glance between you both?"

"You remember the night that Scorpion spoke the first prophecy, the night we saw the news report about Justice's killing spree? The two of us had been here that time as well. We'd stood in front of this font and something had communicated with us. Something incredibly old, incredibly powerful. I think it's what gave Scorp her power."

"Gods! Why can't life be swine-faced simple!" Tigress approached the font, her shoulders bent forward and her body tense, as if the stone bowl would leap forward and attack her. A hint of puzzlement crept to the corners of her mouth. "What's with the inscription?"

"I don't know. Night didn't say."

"Who the hell are the *knaves* and who doesn't want to be responsible for them?"

Dave gave his head a slight shake. "I don't think that really matters. Look at the words; they're an acrostic."

"A what now?"

"The first letters of the message spell a word or, in this case, a name."

Tigress studied the five words and then swore in an ancient tongue. "No, no, no… This can't be right. Night must be mistaken. Why the hell would she want *that*," she pointed to the small girl now playing hide-and-seek in the pews with the giant, lumbering killing machine that was fashioned from clay, "hidden somewhere that has a definite, slap-me-in-the-face-and-look-at-me, connection with Kanor?"

Dave cast his mind back to the last time that he had stood here, that phantasmagorical journey with Scorpion on the night that Nightingale and Marcus had taken him to *Vixen's Den*. Something had dwelt within this place. Something so powerful. It had wanted to give him a gift.

"You will see such wonders. You will talk of many marvels. Things that have been yet are still to be shall dance upon your tongue."

The sandy-haired vampire shuddered as he recalled the soft words that had enticed him, and then his stomach churned in revulsion as he recalled Scorpion burning at the touch of the fiery waters. He had watched her skin pucker and blister as her eyes had melted in her sockets.

So, he had done the right thing. He had refused the gift that he had been offered in order that the entity could save his companion's life. Scorpion had been born anew from the living water and, within her, she held the key to the Prophecies.

"It's the Abyss," he stated. "I don't know how, but it touches our realm here, in this spot. Night said that she encountered something powerful here. Something that destroyed the nave and the roof of the church. This font was placed here when the church was rebuilt. I think it's a portal to the waters that surround us. I think..." and then he stopped as a quiet noise reached his ears. "Do you hear that?"

The three Children of Cain stood perfectly still as the sound of rushing water reached their ears.

"Where the hell is that coming from?" Tigress growled.

They turned as one toward the font.

The voice of an exultant child rang through the suspense. "Mummy!" the Potency squealed. "She's here!"

Then everything changed.

They found themselves standing on a wide, exposed plain. There was no vegetation for miles around. All was barren, bleak.

"I hate it when stuff like this happens," Tigress grumbled, her hand protectively running over the bulge in her satchel. "Where do you think we are?"

Dave shook his head as he studied the empty landscape. "Haven't a clue, but," he said as he looked past Tigress' shoulder, "I think *she* might know."

Into their midst walked a woman. At least they *thought* it was a woman. The being appeared to have assumed a female shape but did not seem to be able to decide exactly what that form should be. It constantly shifted from one thing to another. One moment, a middle-aged 1950s suburban housewife, the next a dark-haired woman wearing a Roman toga, then a female Neanderthal wearing skins of slain animals. Constantly, it shifted through an infinity of female forms throughout the ages. However, there was one thing that most definitely identified her.

"Mummy!"

"My child."

The Potency threw itself at the transforming entity as the ever-shifting female crouched down and opened its loving arms.

The vampires stood and watched as mother and daughter embraced.

"Well, my sweetness, how are you?" The words flowed in a rich feminine contralto like a summer brook caressing the rocks beneath its surface.

"I have been sooooo busy, Mummy. I have seen lots and lots of things and done so much. There have been wolfies, vampires; hot places, cold places. All sorts of people. I even met *him*. You know?" She cast a furtive glance over her shoulder at the Children of Cain. "The one I have to be careful who I talk about. The one of the three."

The manifestation of the primal waters that encircled the Realms nodded. "I know, my sweetness. I have seen that and more." She ran a fluidly changing hand through the long green hair of the weirdling and smiled warmly with affection. "You have been such a good little girl."

The three vampires, as one, glanced at the construct that stood sentinel to the side of the reunion and then shared a knowing collection of raised eyebrows.

The Abyss smiled. "However, I think perhaps your latest toy needs to be put back in its box for now."

The weirdling made to protest, but its mother held up a commanding finger. "No protests. Everything has its time. You and your sister know that."

The child pouted but nodded. "I miss my sister," she sighed as she waved her small fingers and the clay golem sank down into the ground. "I wish that she was here."

"You know that she can't be right now. She is safe. She has her protector."

The Potency nodded and a small smile of recollection touched her lips then faded away. "I know. I know. But still…"

"Anyway," the mother stood, her face shifting from dark to light and back again as she did, her clothes a twin-piece power-dressed suit of the eighties then a flowing silk kimono, "enough of us for now. We have guests." To Dave and Scorpion, she said, "You two I have already met." To Tigress, "You, I believe I have not yet had the pleasure."

The normally fiery redhead swallowed down her unaccustomed nerves and stepped tentatively forward. "The name's Tigress."

"I know. I know all there is to know about you," the woman smiled. "I just said that I hadn't met you yet."

The vampire's usual snappy personality found the strength to reassert itself and she opened her mouth to throw something back at the timeless entity, but a cold hand on her wrist and a shake of Scorpion's head suggested that would not be a wise move.

The Abyss smiled at the blonde. "She's still getting you into bother, I see."

Scorpion shrugged as the shifting entity stepped close and placed a hand on the side of the mute vampire's head. It nodded as it gently caressed her temple. "All as should be. All as should be."

Dave gave a polite cough. "Well, if that is everything, perhaps you would be kind enough to send us back?" He felt a sudden surge of dread as the entity turned its undivided attention toward him. "Please?" he squeaked.

The being's eyes transformed over and over as they studied him. Blue, red, green, yellow, hazel, purest fire. They flickered between the continual shifting of hues and colours. "You have no idea," it eventually whispered almost too low even for the hyper-sensitive hearing of the three vampires. "No idea at all, do you?"

Dave swallowed. "As… as to what?"

The Abyss just smiled and turned away.

"Where do you think we are?" she asked. "Where is this place?"

The vampires gazed again at their surroundings — the bleak, barren landscape with no, vegetation, no habitation — and instinctively they knew.

"We are post-Divergence," Dave stated. "Kanor has risen and the constructs have devastated the land. Humanity is finished."

The edge of a smile touched the entity's lips. She pointed out to the distance, to a small muddy track that seemed to lead to nowhere. "Not quite."

The vampires watched as two small forms came into view on the horizon. It was impossible to make out their features at this angle and distance, but they appeared to be a boy in his early teenage years and a girl of some years younger. They were talking between themselves with the comfortable familiarity of siblings.

"Who are they?" Dave asked.

"Two you will meet. Two you will protect. Two you will lose."

"You couldn't be a bit more specific?"

The Abyss just smiled enigmatically before touching her child on the shoulder. "I believe you have something to say to Mister Nichols?"

The small girl looked up at her mother and frowned.

"A thank you?" the patient parent explained.

The weirdling's lips formed into an "O" of recognition and she ran forwards, throwing herself around the male vampire's legs in a crushing embrace. "Thank you!" she said into the material of his trousers, before peering up at him with her big green orbs. "Thank you for bringing me to my mummy."

"That's okay," Dave shrugged. "Children need their parents." Then he frowned as he felt the brushing of something inside his head. He flinched at what sounded like the report of a gun firing a long way away followed by distant screaming.

The Potency's face fell. "I'm so sorry…" she began.

There was a discreet cough from the child's mother and the Potency slipped her small fingers into Dave's hand, squeezing his cold fingers tight. As she did so, Dave felt ice trickle down his spine and, for a moment, he could have sworn that he could hear the heavy breathing of a dark, terrible beast. The small figure nodded and smiled up at him, a sad glint in her green eyes. "I can't help you with what is going to happen soon, but I promise that I will be there when you need me most," she said.

And, once more, the three vampires were standing in the church of All Saints. The vague hint of old incense hung pleasantly in the air, mingling with the furniture polish that had produced a loving shine to the old wooden pews.

Dave glanced down and saw that, in his hand, he held a green hemispherical stone. He stood by the font and his foot rested on a flagstone that rocked under his weight. He knelt down, pried the flag from its position and lay the stone in the recess underneath. Nodding grimly to himself, he positioned the slab across the sleeping entity, rose to his feet and absentmindedly brushed the dust off the floor from his knees. He turned to the other two vampires. "We've done what we were asked. Let's go."

Tigress' mouth opened in remembrance of something that she had forgotten. "Wait! I want to see the misericords. Nathan created one which…"

The younger vampire held up his hand. "No. Now is not the time."

"But…"

He shook his head as he turned to study the font's inscription one more time. "I don't think we're finished with this place yet. I'm sure we will return. You can show me then. Okay?"

Tigress took a calming pause, then nodded.

The three of them made their way out into the night, carefully closing the oak door behind them. As they did, they were sure that they could hear a threefold tune singing on the night breeze.

November Night

We walk inside the market. Down into the deep clinical depths of alabaster white tiles that hang precariously from ill-maintained tiles. Our footfalls echo around the empty corridors where no customers venture. Even *we* aren't buying, just curious.

The chip shop stands where it always did, two bored girls stare across the desolate counter. I count the Guinea pigs scurrying around behind them, ginger balls of squeaking fur. How many, I ask.

Fifty-one, yawns one of the girls.

Fifty-one *she* shouts, thinking I could not hear.

I ignore *her* and I ask about the two white birds that strut amongst the scurrying rodents, their ibis-like beaks pick, pick picking at the dirty floor. The girl tells me their name but I either do not hear her or immediately lose interest as I am buying two cans of drink (one ginger beer *hers*, one Pepsi Max *mine*) as *she* is thirsty. The girl asks if I want salt and vinegar and I try to explain that we just wanted drinks then turn to see that *she* has finished her drink and is now drinking mine, obliviously.

I am thirsty, so thirsty.

My anger fuels my thirst as *she* talks incessantly about the shops in this new arcade that is a very old one. They are all people that *she* knows, not me. The shops are full of expensive tat that I would never buy but which *she* waxes lyrical about. Stuffed door stops, patchwork coats, things that tinkle as they move.

I make to say that a guy I knew used to own one of these plots. He would be making a killing now if he was still here. He's been dead many years now. But *she* has moved on, bored and uninterested, out of the arcade.

My bags are heavy as I follow along the street, lagging ever behind *her*.

The canvas tote bag digs into my shoulder, and the brown leather bag with far too many pockets is slippery to the touch. It keeps falling from my fingers as middle-aged women walk past, staring at me.

She begins to pull ahead of me and crosses by the war memorial on the green. *She* notices neither the memorial to the dead nor the fact that I am now so far behind as *she* is still talking to me, even though I am not there.

She does not see the photographer snapping the bone-white bookmark stuck to the pitted tar macadam. Eighteen years, he says. Eighteen years it has been here and no one knows how it got there. I hear a squawking as I cross the road and a sharp-eyed bird comes to greet me. It is juvenile and unafraid, its plumage downy. I think it is a corvid of some sort. A raven perhaps but the flashes of blue in its wings state otherwise. A young magpie, but not. Its bright yellow underbelly looks nothing like the magpies that frolic in the trees nearby. The man with the camera informs me of its genus, but I cannot hear his garbled words.

I walk up the road alone, my bags trying to disable me and I spy a small white dog rush into an open garden. Passing the hedge, I see three tan and white bull terriers lounging under an open window making me wonder to whom they belong and does the owner of the house know.

Gold Street is infernally hot as I proceed along the ever-increasing footpath. I consider sitting in one of the many sofas that have been placed on the kerbside. They look comfy and inviting but there are possessions both on them and on their accompanying tables. Extension cables stretch across the footpath into the houses. I decide that they must be resident use only and carry on, spying the familiar petrol station off on my left.

My throat is dry, hoarse like a camel. I remember *she* drank my drink. As *she* is no longer here I choose to buy another. I enter the small paper shop made of bricks and mortar. I do not wear a mask as I know he will not mind. This was the man who sold my father out-of-date chocolate forty-five years ago. Public health is not his main concern. I gaze around the dimness of the un-windowed shop and try to locate the correct fridge amongst the shelves, the sandwiches, the tinned produce and the mess. How can I help you, he asks. I've found it, I say and clamber around and over the obstacles in my way. You need to tell me what you want, he demands. You need to tell me now. I look for the drink but it isn't there. It isn't there, I say. Because you need to tell me what you want so I can write it on my paper.

When he writes it down, I take my drink and pull the tab open with my teeth. I listen to the music on his radio as the tepid liquid spills down my chin. A harmonium

plays a familiar tune and I walk out into the stifling heat,
the bags pulling even heavier on my arms.
    I awake to chilled darkness and despair.

Perchance to Dream

Agnes opened her eyes and, as was her wont in the morning, let out a deep sigh as she just lay there for a few minutes making sure she understood exactly what she had seen. The emphasis was definitely on *seen*. She never tried to *understand*; that was not her job.

When she was satisfied that she had gathered, ordered and correlated all the relevant information, she sat up and started to draw up her list for the day.

Clean oven.

Wash windows.

Book chimney sweep for later in the year.

She paused a moment, looked at what she had just written and shook her head before striking out the last line.

Buy groceries (don't forget butternut squash).

Visit Ethel in Preston.

She was aware of a small furry creature pummelling the duvet next to her. Reaching out, she absent-mindedly stroked the little cat as she re-read her to-do list. Perhaps she ought to book the chimney sweep, just in case?

She shook her head.

No. There would be no need, certainly if the dreams were true.

Later that morning, she sat on the train running down the track between Lancaster and Preston. Agnes didn't drive; she never had. When she'd been growing up, her father had constantly nagged her and nagged her that she ought to learn, that it would be useful for a modern woman, but she had never really seen the need. There were buses, there were bikes, there were trains; why should she have the stress and expense of something mechanical in her life? Lord knew there were far too many things already there to cause her untold anxiety.

Like the dreams.

They had started when she was just a little girl, when her granddad had passed away. The night after they had buried him deep in the dark consuming earth, she had gone to bed very quiet, then buried her face into her pillows and sobbed and sobbed and sobbed. Little Agnes had loved him beyond description and her life would never be the same. No more would she be whisked up onto his bony knee to be told a wild tale of adventures from his youth. No more would she feel the surreptitious press of a boiled sweet into her hand under the dining table, out of the watchful eye of her mother.

Then, as she had lain there in bed, her cheeks wet with tears, she had felt a familiar hand on her shoulder.

She had turned and looked up into the kind face of the man they had just planted in the earth and she had not been afraid. Why should she? It was her granddad. He had sat on the corner of her bed and they had talked about all sorts of things. He had told her not to worry, that everything was going to be okay. He had said that she wouldn't see him anymore, but that she was to remember that he would always love her. He had told her that she would see lots of other things and people at night from now on.

Some of the things that she saw would scare her.

Agnes' eyes drifted out towards Clougha Pike as they zoomed past, and she shuddered. Even now she could see vague images of scaly wings (two red, two black) and the screeching noises of unnatural battle echoed in her ears.

She dragged her mind back to the oven that needed cleaning. She would pick up some *Mister Muscle* on the way home when she did her grocery shopping.

Ethel's house was fortunately not too far away from the train station. Agnes didn't know Preston very well, but the little map app on her phone got her there in no time. As she walked down Connaught Road, she wondered about two things.

The first was the unusual setup of the street. The road was still cobbled and one side had Victorian stone terraced housing. However, the row of houses on the other side was a bright, contrasting redbrick terrace. She didn't really travel to Preston much. Most of what she needed was in Lancaster. In her home town, the streets were either Victorian or post second world war. It was very rare that you got a mix. If you did, then the modern was *properly* modern and did not try to replicate the building style of a hundred years previous. Here though, it was as if an architect had come along and said, "I really like what we've got going on here, but let's just update the building materials." Or, perhaps both sides of the street had been built at the same time with one construction crew favouring brick and the other stone? Agnes guessed she would never know.

Just like she probably wouldn't get the chimney swept later that year.

The second thing she pondered was how Ethel would take to her visit. As she approached the uPVC door set in the Victorian stonework, Agnes considered that there were two general responses of those that she visited: come on in, go the hell away. If it was the second, then that was that and there was nothing that she could do. She would have tried to deliver the message and she would have failed. The person that had sent her would be upset but understanding and Agnes would move on, leaving it behind her, awaiting her next visitor.

This happened about two times out of ten. She guessed it was an acceptable average, all things considered.

She knocked on the door and waited. It opened and a woman about twenty years older than her peered through the gap between the door and the frame. The householder frowned at the stranger on her doorstep, obviously trying to work out if she was either trying to sell something or rob her blind.

"Good morning, are you Ethel Ashworth?"

The woman nodded silently.

Agnes took a steadying breath.

"I've got a message for you. It's from Dick, your late husband."

So, it had been a *come on in* response and now Agnes was sitting in Ethel's small living room sipping a perfectly brewed cup of tea that had been served in the best china which was obviously kept reserved for special guests.

Like those people who claimed to have been talking to her dead husband.

"So," Agnes began, with her usual rehearsed introduction, "first, thank you for not shutting the door in my face. Second, you must have questions. Please feel free to ask them."

The octogenarian just looked at her for a moment, her cup of tea held in her hands. Agnes could tell that the elderly woman was trying to think of the right thing to ask, but couldn't quite formulate the words into the right order.

She decided to fill in the gaps and the growing awkward silence.

"My name is Agnes Broadbent. I've lived in Lancaster all my life. When I was six, my grandfather died. The night after we buried him, he came to me in a dream to tell me that everything would be okay. Ever since then, other recently deceased people have visited me, asking me to pass messages on to their nearest and dearest."

"You say my Dick came to see you?"

Agnes nodded.

"How can I trust you?"

"When you were first courting, he used to take you to Haslam Park all the time, didn't he?"

Ethel stared at her with a good dose of scepticism in her eyes. "Most folks did back in those days. No television as such. Just saying that doesn't mean he told you that."

"No, it doesn't. But there was the time that you stayed out too late there because he'd forgotten to wind his watch that day. You had to get ready for work the next morning. It was going to be your first day working at the hardware store on Friargate. Your dad had arranged it; if you were late home, he would have gone ballistic. So, Dick snuck you home and helped you climb up the out-house and in through your bedroom window."

The elderly woman's face was motionless.

"It was your own private little story. Something you used to tell each other whenever you were feeling sad or troubled. You never told anyone else and neither did he.

"Until last night."

Ethel set her cup and saucer down on her coffee table and picked up a small photo frame that sat there. In it was a picture of a young man and woman smiling back at the photographer. "He was everything to me," she said. "My absolute life. I don't know what I'm supposed to do without him."

Agnes took a steadying breath. "Well, that's the thing. Dick has sent a very specific instruction for you, and you might not like what he has to say.

"Stop annoying everyone around you.

"He says that you need to learn to stand on your own two feet. You can't keep depending on everyone else. They all have their own lives and troubles. He says that you're fit and healthy and still have all your marbles (his words, not mine) and that you need to take respons-ibility for your own life.

"If you don't, you're going to end up a lonely old wo-man with no friends. You've already driven away the Johnsons down the road. He can't understand why you rang them up at three in the morning to say that your heat-ing was making *a funny noise*. Plus, there was last week with the young couple at twenty-three. Telling them that you didn't like the colour of their new bedroom wallpaper was not a sensible thing to do, was it?

"He wants you to remember the young woman that was giggling manically as she shimmied up the window frame to squeeze into the small bedroom window way past her bedtime. You may not be that age anymore and you definitely don't have the strength or agility to do that again, but you still have the spunk inside of you (again, his words, not mine). So, don't go all feeble and needy on everyone because, in the end, they'll just walk away and you'll have no idea why they were all *mean* to you."

Agnes set her half-drunk cup of tea down on a mother-of-pearl coaster and stood up. "Anyway, that's all I was asked to tell you. I'll see myself out."

She turned and walked out of the house, leaving the old woman with her thoughts and memories.

Agnes chose an unoccupied table seat on her train ride back to Lancaster, eschewing the company of other travellers in the carriage. She wanted some time alone with her own thoughts. As the seat opposite her was un-occupied, she allowed herself to stretch her legs out as she gazed out of the window, the Lancashire countryside whipping past.

Had she been too harsh on the old woman? Per-haps, but then she was just the messenger, wasn't she? The dear departed husband had presented her with the message and she had just been there to deliver it. It was up to the widow to make of the words what she wanted.

Clougha drew up on the right, its craggy top bright in the spring sunshine. The warmth caressed Agnes' face and she felt her eyelids start to relax, to droop…

They fought, as always, above the top of the Pike. One red dragon with seven heads, one dark obsidian black. Each unearthly beast screamed as they merci-

lessly gouged each other with sharp talons. Their shrieks and roars echoed across the land.

Until there was silence and two different figures stood atop the hill. One, with a gentle face and soft brown hair, said goodbye to the other and turned to join a small group of fairy folk that had gathered around him. They walked off towards a glowing, pulsing disk of purple light through which they stepped and vanished.

The other, left alone, bent and picked up two items, a chalice and a sword. He lifted them in his hands and, as he did, a bright nimbus emanated from his body and splendid white wings tinged with flickering flames unfurled from his shoulders, bearing him up into the burning sky. A song older than time itself resonated through the super-heated air and, as Agnes watched in terror, all creation seemed to implode towards him.

She woke, as she always did from this dream, with a juddering start.

There was a man sitting across from her. Although his hair was greatly receding, he looked to be in his late thirties. He sported a neatly trimmed beard and grey eyes twinkled through a pair of small, steel-rimmed spectacles. He wore black clericals and a small dog collar was positioned at his throat.

"You appear to have been having a dream, my dear," came a well-spoken Scottish lilt.

Agnes glanced around the carriage at the other occupants who were all apparently sitting frozen in time.

"I think, perhaps, that I still am," she replied. She looked at her companion. "Do you have a message for a loved one?"

"Indeed I do," he replied. "And it concerns all that you saw as you dozed just now."

Agnes started. "What is his name?"
The deceased clergyman told her.
"What is the message?"
He told her that as well.
She felt a chill down in her stomach.
"From whom should I say the message has come?"
A genuine, warm smile touched his lips.
"Tell him it's from Spliff."

Author's Notes

Greetings reader and thank you not only for purchasing this, my seventh little anthology of short horror and urban fantasy stories but also for carrying on to the part of the book that is ignored by about ninety per cent of readers. (Okay, I made that statistic up, but it's probably true. Let's face it most folks have now either nipped to the loo, gone to pick the kids up from school or wandered off to put the kettle on…)

As I sit here wondering what little anecdotes and factoids I can regale you with regarding the eight tales you've just read, I find it rather apt that (as I write this, at least) it's the day before Halloween. It's the day that the clocks have gone back, so my body clock has given me an extra hour to stare blankly out of my study window at the pitch black of a cold, wet October morning. Tomorrow is the day when many people celebrate the world of the supernatural. Weather permitting, kids will be knocking on doors, hassling perturbed pensioners for treats and glowing pumpkin heads will be festooned around the city. In this modern world, Halloween, the Eve of All Hallows, has become sanitised, homogenised and well and truly capitalised. Back in the day, the pagan festival Samhain marked the end of the season of Light and the coming of the Darker times of the year. Later on, in the ninth century, it was assimilated into the Christian calendar with the first of November becoming All Hallows (All Saints) and the evening before becoming synonymous with things that were far less *saintly*. So Halloween became the day for vampires, werewolves, ghosties and goblins — all the beasties and monsters that would cry for release from *out of the depths*…

Family History

This story about the archaeologist Robert Richmond is the first of the four shorts in this anthology that are directly part of the ever-expanding Spallucciverse. The others are *Knocking At The Door, Family Reunion* and *Perchance To Dream. Christmas Fear* might also be in the same world, but I'm not too sure about that yet. (More on that later).

There are certain characters in the Spallucciverse that have been around for a long time now. Sam (obviously), Grace, Spliff, Lucifer and Alec to name but a few. However, there are certain others who were even around before I wrote *Casebook* back in 2011. Professor Richmond is one of these. Along with his daughter, Eloise, he featured in the latest draft of my as-yet-unpublished magnum opus, *Fallen Angel,* when I wrote that back in about 2005. There is a scene there where Eloise visits her father at the insistence of her boyfriend, the central character of the book. It is revealed to the reader that Richmond is in fact in possession of the Cup, which he dug up on a recent archaeological venture. *Family History* prepares the way for this scene as well as a story in the eighth Sam Spallucci book *Lux Æterna* (due out in 2023), where Sam and the vampire Dave Nichols go in search of the Blade.

Those of you who are constant readers of Sam's adventures will be fully aware that Sam is a great fan of Richmond and his acerbic style. Also, if you are sharp-eyed and have read 2022's *Sam Spallucci: Fury of the Fallen*, you may have noticed that the chat show on which he appears is the one that Sam and Asherah watch during *The Case of the Spurned Siren*. Not only that, but we find out here what the responsibilities are that the Power called Dagan refers to in the same case during the encounter with Asmodeus.

I thoroughly enjoyed writing this one, especially as it crosses over with numerous other stories, paving the way for *Fallen Angel*, the events of which have begun to be set in motion by the time of *Fury of the Fallen*. The other story that does the same in this anthology is *Family Reunion*, but more on that later.

Christmas Fear

About three years ago, I was approached to write a Christmas-themed horror story for a blog. The original version of *Christmas Fear* was the result. At the time, I felt it was a bit of a rush job. I liked the premise of the story and how it panned out, but I felt it was just lacking something. As a result, I let it be published online but then filed it away in the "*look at again later*" folder on my computer.

When I came to working on *Out Of The Depths* I felt this little short calling to me from literary limbo. I opened it up, dusted it down and went in with a fresh pair of eyes, tidying things up and producing something that I was much happier with.

Christmas is supposed to be a time for festivity and happiness. Families are supposed to come together and enjoy each other's company around large meals and all that jazz. However, for many individuals, Christmas can be a terribly upsetting time, especially if they've lost a loved one. For a number of years, I was one of these people. As I've talked about before in other books, my father suffered from crippling rheumatoid arthritis. On the Christmas Eve of my nineteenth year, I was away on a church placement when I received a phone call that he had suffered a heart attack and had been rushed into hospital. His body had started to give in to the illness that had plagued him for most of my life and he was dead in just over a month's time. It has taken many years for me to, once again, see Christmas as a time for celebration. Some people never reclaim the joy that they may have once had for that time of year.

Although *Christmas Fear* is a stand-alone short, it could very well be part of the Spallucciverse. The creature that poses as Buster does seem similar to the tentacled creature from the other dimension in *Fury of the Fallen*'s *The Case of the Bothersome Books*. Not everything supernatural has to cross Sam's path.

Knocking At the Door

This short story, with the slaughtering of the poor Hesketh family, is a direct cross-over with *Fury of the Fallen*. It is, as it were, a behind-the-scenes peek at the events that transpired before Sam arrived at their house with the Potency.

Their house is actually based on a house that used to feature quite a lot in my dreams. On many occasions, I found myself walking up to this old battered white house and walking down an incredibly long hallway before emerging out the other end, normally into a garden of some type. Here I took that house and combined it with what must be one of the greatest fears for a homeowner, a home invasion. I cranked it up to eleven by having the invader being a sociopathic fallen angel.

Maisie

As a teenager, I was a huge fan of the British comic *2000AD*. Back in the 1980s, there was a Future Shock story entitled *One Man's Meat*. This story was in itself inspired by Philip K Dick's *Beyond Lies The Wub* and both tales centre around the character of the tale eating a sentient creature which then takes over their body. *Maisie* is my homage to both of these classics.

Date Night

This is actually the oldest of the stories in this anthology. I originally wrote it back in 2012 with the intention of it being included in *Oh Taste And See*. However, the book proved to be too long so a couple of stories had to be shelved. *Date Night* was one of them. I then intended to use it in *Mourning Has Broken* but it was too similar in feel to *Frank's Castle*, so it was passed over once again. It has now finally seen the light of day.

The inspiration for the story was a house that I used to visit a lot when I was a student. Underneath it was this huge, creepy cellar that stretched the full length of the building. It was quite easy to imagine all manner of nefarious deeds taking place there. In fact, the same house was used in *Sam Spallucci: Ghosts From The Past* as the residence of Caroline Adamson. That time, the cellar was used by Malcolm Wallace when he sent the son of Sam and Caroline to Beyond.

Family Reunion

This is probably my personal favourite from this anthology. Not only does it contain the vampires Scorpion and Tigress, who are two of my favourite creations, but also the Potency. First appearing in *Bloodline* and then being fleshed out more in *Fury*, the sociopathic stone from the dawn of time is just so much fun to work with. I genuinely spend all my time grinning like a loon when I create her dialogue. Although I really would not have wanted to share a four-hour car journey with her. The vamps have my deepest sympathy there.

Like *Family History*, this is a serious piece of crossover work. First, it serves as a sort of epilogue to *Fury* as we see what happens to the Potency after she leaves Sam. Also, it refers back to Scorp and Tigress spending time with the woodcarver Nathan in the short story *Memento* which first appeared in *Let All Mortal Flesh* and then in the *Children of Cain* omnibus. However, the biggest crossover has to be with *Fallen Angel*. There is a scene where it is discovered that All Saints has been broken into and the statue of the Madonna and Child has been stolen. This story takes place directly before that scene.

But it doesn't stop there...

The loose flagstone by the font is referred to in the Nightingale story *Songbird* and also the Alec story *Child of Light* which is due out in 2023. Not only that but we finally meet the personification of the Abyss, the sentient river that flows between the three Realms. From this point on she will play an increasingly prominent role in the events leading up to the Divergence, featuring in Sam's adventures and the final two books in the Bobby Normal series.

November Night

I suffer from a condition called Meniere's Disease. It is an inner ear imbalance that causes, amongst other things, continual noises and tinnitus. When I was younger, the condition was completely out of control and I used to have the most incredibly vivid dreams and night-mares as my brain tried to make sense of the random noises it was receiving. Another symptom, as can be present in many long-term illnesses, can be paranoia, es-pecially when the illness isn't properly managed. When you mix all this up into one big phantasmagorical cooking pot, you end up with things like *November Night*.

I'm not sure exactly when I had this dream, but I must have scribbled it down when I woke up the next morning as I came across the barely legible scrawl a few months ago. After deciphering the ramblings, I tidied it up and formed it into possibly my most surreal short to date.

Perchance to Dream

This little short is effectively the prologue to *Sam Spallucci: Lux Æterna*, which I am currently writing. I feel that it really speaks for itself and doesn't need much in the way of explanation. It was one of those stories that, like many of my novels, began with its ending. I knew that I wanted to have Spliff appear to a medium, it was just a case of letting the story evolve and grow until I reached that point.

Anyway, I hope you enjoyed these little notes.

A.S.Chambers

Take care and keep looking for what lurks in the shadows.

ASC October 2022

About The Author

A.S.Chambers resides in Lancaster, England. He lives a fairly simple life of walking in the countryside, gazing at mountains and rescuing his cat from the dastardly machinations of net curtains.

He is quite happy for, and in fact would encourage, you to follow him on Facebook, Instagram and Twitter.

There is also a nice, shiny website:
www.aschambers.co.uk